To Lucas and Brandon. Thank you for making this book come to life.

PROLOGUE:

Kasimira looked at her daughter, "Roza, don't play with that!" she laughed and scooped up the one year old girl, plucking the vial of blue powder from her hand. The baby giggled and grabbed at her mother's dress. Kasimira hugged her child and smelled the sweet scent of grass and parchment, the very same scents that filled their home. From a distance, she heard a cry, and sighing, went into the back room, where her daughter's twin brother had been napping.

"Oh, Rowan, whatever shall I do with you?" she picked him up in the other arm and viewed both of her children, "You two are in cahoots to drive me mad, aren't you?" Rowan stuck out his hand and began to play with Roza's white hair. Kasimira laughed, "Crazy babies." and sighed, *If only they would nap for more than half an hour,* she thought longingly, *then I might get something done around here.* Although she was royalty, she had no staff to take care of the children or of the small castle they resided in. This was a remote island, and it was the only place to keep the children safe. If people knew who they were...they'd be killed for sure. What would she do then? What would Sean do?

She told herself not to worry. The castle was well-hidden. No one would find them. Who would think of the dark island that was rumored to be exactly that, a rumor? Even the natives who lived on the island hadn't bothered them. A peaceful bunch, they were. If you didn't bother them, they wouldn't bother you, seemed to be the general rule of the land. And while Sean was trading daily with the men, Kasimira went weekly to seek the women for help with raising her children. They'd become sort of friends. They were always so interested in her garb and perfumes, for they wore, well, quite little, and they certainly didn't want their scent to be carried around in the air due to prey and possible invaders with animals.

Roza struck Rowan on the head, sick of having her hair played with. Rowan sniffled and started to cry. Roza didn't even pay attention, for she was too busy musing at the patterns on her mother's dress. "Roza Kiara Collins! Do not hit your brother!" Kasimira put Roza in her cot and left her to play with her silver bell as she comforted Rowan and sang softly to him.

"Kas! Kassi!" Kasimira put a now-calm Rowan into his cot, handed him a silver rattle, and went to greet her husband in the huge foyer of the castle, "How was trading?" Sean smiled, "Better than usual. They've found a new family of deer to the North." Kasimira smiled and walked to the cook room where Sean set down his large bag and took her by the waist, "How is my beautiful wife?" Kasimira caressed his face and smiled, "Wonderful, as usual, but tired. Your daughter is determined never to take a nap." Sean chucked, "Well, why don't we go see her? I'm sure we can tire her out somehow."

They went into the nursery and found both children asleep. Around both of them was a white glow tinted with color. Rowan's glow seemed more gold, while Roza's seemed to be almost red. Kasimira went over to cover Rowan with a blanket while Sean stood over Roza with a worried glance.

"Sean, let's go rest. They're going to be up all night at this rate." Sean chuckled, and then his face became serious, "Kasimira, what do you think will become of our little girl?" Kasimira gave him a concerned look, "What do you mean?" Sean sighed and took his wife's hand, "Her glow is tinted with red. She is prophesied to become Dark. The both of them together...they will destroy each other again. I don't know what we would do if that happened. Perhaps it would be best if they were to be apart. They wouldn't have the chance to fight, to become enemies. They could hone their skills." Kasimira was appalled, "Sean, we can't keep them apart. They belong together! They're twins! They're two halves of a whole. They need each other." Sean looked at the two sleeping children with concern, "Kasimira, think of their safety. She's already becoming violent. I love her as much as you do, but they have to be safe. We need to figure something out." Kasimira tore her hands away from his, "Violent? She's just feisty. All children are. They will not end up like the others. They're Rowan and Roza. Not Faemin and Listow." and with a last glance at the children, Kasimira left.

Sean sighed. What were they to do? Of course they weren't Faemin and his brother, but shouldn't they take every precaution to ensure the safety of their children? What if people found where they were hiding? What if they found out what the children really were? They had to learn how to control themselves and their power. It was key to the safety of the whole country. Placing a kiss on Roza's head, he left the children's room and went to bed himself.

—

"You will go to the East wing, and I will take the west. Basa and Ranma have their troops set around the top and in the secret passageways." the man in black nodded and gave a signal to the five men in the same black uniform behind him. In a flash, they were gone.

—

"Sean...Sean...do you hear that?" Kasimira shook her husband lightly, her eyes still closed. Sean sighed, "No." Kasimira moaned, and just as she was about to fall into a deep sleep once again, there was the creak of their heavy bedroom door opening. Sean and Kasimira both bolted awake. Sean grabbed his sword and Kasimira grabbed for her daggers. Standing in front of them were five people dressed all in black, their eyes the only visible part of their bodies.

"Who are you?" demanded Sean, "What do you want?" one of the people in black stepped forward, "You." and before they knew what had happened, the king and queen were unconscious.

Sean opened his eyes. At first, everything was dark, and then slowly, shapes and shadows turned into colors and pictures and a room. It was their own dungeon. He suddenly realized what had happened, and tried to stand and run forward, but chains and shackles kept tied to the floor. He tugged at the biting metal and shouted in frustration. He looked around himself for the first time and saw Kasimira lying on the floor across the room from him.

"Kasimira! Kasimira!" he shouted to her, but she did not answer. Out of the shadows came a voice, "She will not wake up. She is already gone." Sean didn't understand, "Gone? What do you mean, gone?" The voice became a man dressed in black as he stepped out of the shadows, and he looked at the woman lying on the floor. "She is no longer with us, Your Highness."

Sean felt his whole body sag to the floor as he realized what the man meant. "What do you want?" he managed to ask. The man shrugged, "It's simple, really. We want your children. And we don't want you interfering with our plans." Sean felt a rage surge through his veins, "Leave my children alone! Aah!" There was a second of pain and breathlessness, and it was cold.

The man in black sighed. It really would have been much easier if he had just stayed unconscious. No matter. He was gone now, and there was nothing that stood in their way. He was, in fact, very pleased with himself. The little monsters were in his hands, now.

"Sir! Sir! The children are gone!" the man in black looked to the stairwell, where one of his soldiers was panting. "What?" he exclaimed, "What is this nonsense you speak, man?" the soldier caught his breath, "The children aren't here."

The man in black looked at his dead prisoners as the reality sunk over him. He screamed in rage, "Find them! Find them now! I will NOT have these monstrosities roaming free!"

And so the search began.

CHAPTER 1:

"I don't understand, Garren. Why must I go to live with the wolves?" the king picked up the little white-haired girl, set her on his lap, and tickled her. "Because, silly girl, it's who you are! You take the form of one. You must learn to be a wolf. When you are ready, you will return." Roza touched his face, "But no one else can turn into an animal. Why can I?" the king chuckled, "Full of questions, aren't you, little one? It is because you are very special, Roza. You have a gift. Never let anyone tell you differently."

A hunched old man appeared at the doorway. He was scraggly and wrinkled, tanned from the sun. His eyes bored into her, piercing her thoughts with their golden gaze. Roza buried herself into Garren's chest. "Who is that?" she whispered. The king set her down and stood up, "Ah, Dire. Right on time. This is Roza." he took the little child's shoulders and ushered her to stand in front of him. "Roza, this is Dire. He is the leader of the pack in Alacrast." Roza gasped. Alacrast, the Dark Land? She was being sent there? A tear streamed down her face, "Garren, I don't want to go. I want to stay here with you and Ana, please! Don't send me to Alacrast!" the king got onto one knee and took her hands, "It is only for a very short time. Before you know it, you'll be back. I promise. Be my big girl?" Roza was torn. She was supposed to go with this stranger to a cursed land? What if she was hurt? What would she do? With a sigh, she reluctantly nodded and looked at her scraggly teacher. He smiled a sharp-toothed smile. Roza flinched, but she went with him anyway.

Once they were out of the castle, Dire bore a scowl. "You are to do what you are told without question. This is not a time to have fun or to play jokes. You will be trained to be a wolf, and you will make your way up the ranks like everyone else, understood?" Roza was about to cry, and he sensed that, "There will also be no incessant crying! Crying is for the weak, do you understand?" Roza wiped her tears and nodded. "Good," he muttered.

—

"Do you really think this was a wise idea, Garren?" Ana looked up from her needlepoint and gave her husband a concerned look. Garren sighed, "It was Sean's wish for them to be able to control themselves. Rowan is already doing marvelous with his studies and his magic. Roza just needs to be able to control her strength and instincts." Ana shook her head, "They are seven years old, Garren. They should be children, not soldiers." Garren sighed, "They don't have that option, Ana. We have to do what is best for everyone, we must look at the bigger picture. I want them to be happy as much as you do, but they need to be able to control themselves if we ever hope to have such a luxury." Ana set down her loom angrily, "Our life is filled with luxury, you would think there would be something that we can do." Garren shook his head, "Not in this case. They are quite extraordinary children." Ana exhaled and shook her head, "I know."

—

"Do you know how to turn into your wolf form?" inquired Dire. It was the first thing he'd directed towards her in the three days they'd been traveling. Roza nodded and ran, faster than any normal human could run, and felt her legs become paws and her nose elongate. She felt the rush of wind in her hair all over her body and knew she was a wolf. When she looked beside her, she saw an old but wise-looking wolf staring into the distance. He climbed onto a rock and howled. "Welcome to the pack," he cackled.

Within seconds, dozens of wolves appeared from the shadows and bushes. They were covered in different paints, colors that matched their eyes. Most of them had yellow designs, some had orange. Roza didn't know what to do. She was scared, they were all glaring at her. Dire sensed her fear and looked at her angrily, "Fear? We are wolves! We are fearless!" Roza nodded slightly. *Don't fear, don't fear.*

"Roza, this is your new family. Be good." and with that, he sauntered off to converse with other wolf men.

Roza didn't know what to do. She stood there, uncertain, until a small wolf came up to her with a scowl on his face, "You smell funny. Are you really a wolf?" Roza shook her head, "I'm a human." the wolf became enraged, "Human! Traitor! You will kill us!" Roza squealed in fear as he tackled her to the ground, "No! No!" the wolf laughed, "You're a human! I don't care what you say!" Roza growled, "Human? Look at me! It's obvious that I'm more than human, you idiot!" she mustered up the strength to push him off and get up, "Look, I'm just like everyone else here. I'm here for training, and that's all. Now leave me alone." and she sauntered off into the woods.

As soon as she was certain that she was far enough away from the pack, and transformed into a human again, covered in the raggedy clothes she had left in. She sighed and sat down on the ground. What was she to do? Everyone would hate her. They may fear her at home, but they would openly hate her here. Why was everyone so wary of her? Did she look funny? Was it her odd-colored white hair? Perhaps it was her green eyes that made people nervous. Green eyes were very rare in Lodos. Most everyone had brown or blue eyes. Green eyes meant magic. People feared magic.

Off in the distance, Roza could have sworn she heard something. It shouted like shouting. She stood up and ran to follow it. She could hear it clear now, it was the sound of two boys fighting playfully. She stopped when she discovered the edge of the forest and could see a small village. There were children playing all around, but the shouting had come from two very well-dressed boys that were trying to tackle each other. One was older, brown-haired and tan-skinned with dark blue eyes. The younger one was blonde, with crystal blue eyes. They were both clad in blue and gold tunics that were finely embroidered, accompanied by leather boots. Roza gawked at them. She'd never seen another country's garb.

"Who are you?" a little girl, about three years old, tugged on her tunic. Roza exclaimed in surprise, and the boys looked at her. Roza gasped and tried to run, but the little girl ran after her. "No!" Roza cried over her shoulder, "Don't follow me, go home!" and then she heard, "Anna! Come back!" it was one of the boys. Roza stopped and hid behind a tree. The boy finally caught up to the little girl and scooped her up, "Anna! Don't go into the woods, there are wolves in there!" he looked around, "Girl? Girl, come out, don't be afraid. I won't hurt you. I'm sorry about Anna." Roza didn't make a sound. Who knows what Dire would do if he found out she was conversing with humans? She knew how he felt about them, based onto the feelings he'd instilled into the pack. When he received no reply, the boy gave up, went home, and so did Roza.

"The first lesson of today is pouncing. The element of surprise. We must not let our prey know that we are here. You find a place where you cannot be seen, stay silent, crouch, and pounce at the last possible second!" Dire instructed the young pups. The usual class of four had a newcomer, Roza, who looked like she was about to cry. He growled inwardly in disdain. What a weakling, and she was to be his ward? Disgrace.

"Victor, why don't you try? Pounce on Luna." Luna, who was distracted with a butterfly, didn't even hear his command. The pup who had tackled Roza the day before chuckled evilly, "No problem." and crept into the grass behind her. Within seconds, there was a squeal, and Luna was on the ground, surprised, and Victor was laughing. Dire smiled maliciously, "Well done, Victor." Luna got up, "Wait, what are we doing?" Victor rolled his eyes, and another male pup laughed. The last male pup gave her a flirtatious glance, "Pouncing. On top of each other." Luna rolled her eyes and raised a paw, "Can I have a partner that isn't Tallah?" Tallah pretended to be hurt, "Why, Luna, the light of my eyes, the love of my life, you scorn me so?" Luna rolled her eyes again.

"Now, Roza, why don't you give it a try? Pounce on Victor." Roza gulped and looked at Victor, who was giving her a glare. She crept into the grass behind him, and took a few deep breaths. She could do this. She crouched down, and waited long enough to hear Luna ask if she'd ran away. With a silent jump she leapt forward and landed on the ground with an, "Oof!"

Victor growled, "Idiot! You shouldn't take such deep breaths. I could hear you." And under his breath he added, "Typical human." Dire nodded, "Absolutely right, Victor. You were breathing too loud. You must remember that a wolf has very sensitive hearing, and to be silent is the key. That is all for today." Roza sat up and sighed. She was sure she'd had it.

"Um...it's Roza, right?" Luna tapped Roza's shoulder. Roza jumped, and then nodded. Luna shrugged, "I'm not that great at doing things like hunting or pouncing either. That's why the girls take care of the family." Roza gave her a questionable look, "But why shouldn't we be able to do what they can? We're just as good as the boys. We shouldn't be dumbed down because we're girls. That's stupid." Luna looked to the ground and said nothing, so Roza walked away. She wanted Ana and Garren to comfort her. It was so lonely here. No one really liked her, not that Roza cared, it was just that at least at home she had Ana and Garren. Here she had no one.

Before she knew it, she'd arrived at the edge of the forest near the village again. She transformed into her human form once again. She saw the boy from the day before with his friend, playing a game with wooden swords.

"One day," the boy cried, "I'm going to be a mighty king! I'll be just like Father! I'll rule all of Myra and all the other kings will fear me!" the other boy parried his thrust, "Not if I have a say in it, brother. I'm the eldest, which means I'll take the crown!" Martin countered him back, "Not according to Father! Father says the battle will be based on strength and valor alone!" Justin shrugged and laughed mockingly, "Then why even bother? We all know I'll win that!" he looked to his brother, who had sat down and was drawing designs in the dirt with his finger, "Are you alright?" Martin shrugged, "I don't know, Justin. I just feel like I'm destined for something greater, some big adventure." he creased his brow, "Speaking of feelings, do you feel as though we're being...watched?" Justin laughed, "Perhaps it's your ghost girl from yesterday." Martin punched his brother in the shoulder, "I'm serious, Justin! She was no ghost girl, she was as real as you are. I wonder who she is." Justin shrugged and leaned up against a tree, "Probably some illegitimate child being kept in hiding in the woods. Don't fret on her." Martin sat down and started to play with a twig in the dirt, "She seemed so sad, Justin. So lonely. I want to ease her pain."

Justin snorted, "You want to ease everyone's pain. The cook's, the servants', the stable hands', our fathers', everyone's. You're such a goody two shoes, Martin." Martin threw a handful of dirt at his brother, "No, I'm not!" Roza couldn't suppress her giggle at the absurd face that Justin made when the dirt touched his tunic. "What was that?" Martin stood up, his face alert, his senses abuzz. Justin brushed his tunic, "What was what?"

"It was a high-pitched noise, like a giggle, I'm sure of it," Martin came closer to the forest, and Roza sunk further into the bushes, afraid that he would see her again. She had to run, she had to go, but first she needed a distraction. Roza gasped as she stepped on something fuzzy, and cringed as she found it was a rabbit's back leg. She picked up the rabbit, set him down in the opposite direction, and scared it off.

"Whoa!" Martin cried as something ran under his legs. He whirled around, "What was that?" Justin howled with laughter, "It was a rabbit! A rabbit! You, the great, mighty Martin, were startled by a rabbit!" he was almost in tears, clutching his stomach. Martin's cheeks flamed red, "I was not startled! He merely took me by surprise!" when his brother couldn't stop laughing, Martin groaned, "Oh, come on, let's go inside. I'm starving." and with a series of quiet chuckles, Justin followed him.

Roza breathed out a sigh of relief. He was gone. Now she could go without fear of being caught.

"A little close there, don't you think?" Roza whirled around. It was Victor in his human form. She scowled, "I don't know what you mean." Victor glared at the town, "A little too close to humans." Roza raised an eyebrow, "Look at yourself. You're human." Victor shook his head, "This is a curse. The curse of a werewolf, to be able to be a filthy human." he spat on the ground. Roza rolled her eyes, "If humans are so horrible, why did you transform into one? Why didn't you stay a wolf?" Victor came a step closer to her, "Dire sent me to find you. We can't be wolves around the humans, they'll kill us without a thought. We have to be careful. At least you have the sense for that." Roza's eyes widened. Dire? What if Victor told him where she was, what she was doing? He would have her skin.

"You can't tell him the truth!" she pleaded. Victor gave her a disgusted look, "What do you mean? I have to. I have no choice. You're a traitor!" Roza shook her head, "No! Please, I'll do anything! Just don't tell him! I can't disappoint Garren." A corner of Victor's mouth twitched, "Oh that's right, your precious papa." Roza grabbed his tunic collar and brought his face close to hers, "Don't you dare speak against him." and for a moment, Victor felt a twinge of uncertainty. This girl meant business. He pulled away from her, "Whatever. Just...don't come back here,

and I won't tell on you." Roza nodded, "Okay. I won't."
Victor nodded, and without a word, left.

Roza followed him after a while, transforming into a
wolf once again. She was beginning to get used to the
walking-on-four-paws, drinking-with-your-tongue, eating-
without-hands-or-utensils thing, although she missed the
human way of life. What did Victor have against humans,
anyway? They weren't so bad. They could be closed-
minded at times, but once they were open, they were
rational creatures, weren't they? Even if they weren't, what
was she to do? She was supposed to be training to be a great
wolf. How could she ever match up to Victor, who was
born for the wolf lifestyle?

"Hey!" a sultry voice cooed next to her ear. Roza
snapped out of her daydream and looked to where the voice
had come from, "Oh, Tallah, it's you," she said softly.
Tallah winked, "Whatcha doing?" Roza shrugged,
"Walking. Thinking." she sighed sadly. Tallah stepped in
front of her, stopping her in her path, "Hey, are you okay?
Victor was sent to find you, and he came back all angry.
Did he rough you up?" Roza shook her head, "No, I'll just
never match up to him." Tallah laughed, "No one can
match up to Victor, and he's so conceited anyway." Roza
raised an eyebrow, "You call him conceited?" Tallah rolled
his eyes with a smile, "Yeah, okay, well, I can't help it. I'm
gorgeous." and for the first time, Roza laughed. Tallah gave
her a crooked smile, "Your laugh is pretty." Roza could feel
herself almost blush, and then she thought of something.

"Tallah, could you teach me?" Tallah narrowed his eyes, confused and suspicious, "What do you mean, Rosebud?" Roza ignored the nickname and smiled, "Teach me to be a wolf. The lessons that Dire teaches. Pouncing, hunting, pillaging, those kind of things. Teach me!" Tallah was uncertain, "I don't know, I mean, the chief might get suspicious if suddenly you get good." Roza snorted, "I'm just catching up! Come on, if I'm going to be stuck here for who knows how long I might as well do something productive."

With a reluctant grin, Tallah sighed, "I suppose." Roza squealed, "Yes!" and Tallah gave her a look. "Ah-hem, I mean, thanks, Tallah." she tried to be cool, and Tallah just snorted and laughed. Roza swiped him in the shoulder, and laughed with him.

—

"Okay, you ready?" Luna, her new little sister, Azure, and Kenai barked in response to Victor's call. Victor looked at Roza and Tallah with a smile, "Let's get them, guys!" and with a battle cry, the six wolves charged at each other.

"Whoa, whoa, whoa!" their babysitter, Cadence, stopped them just before they crashed into each other, "What are you doing?" Victor became grumpy and Tallah laughed, "We're just playing humans and wolves. We're fighting now. Luna, Az, and Kenai just got done hunting, killing, and eating us." Cadence sighed, "Guys, come on. Can't you be like normal little wolves? Exploring the woods, practicing your pouncing?" Luna sighed, "Come on,

Az, let's go home. Kenai, you coming?" Kenai, who was crazy for Luna, nodded without a second thought. "What about you guys?" she asked Victor, Tallah, and Roza. The three friends looked at each other, "Nah," Victor finally said, "We're going to stick around here." Luna shrugged, "Suit yourself."

"So, what's the plan for today? Want to go sneak on the humans?" Roza asked excitedly. Victor and Tallah gave each other a look. Roza had taught them all about humans, the good humans, that is, and they'd made a habit out of teasing the two that Roza used to sneak on, Martin and Justin. "Sure," they said.

The three made their way to the edge of the forest, where the village was. "So, Tallah, who are you taking to the Blue Moon Feast?" Roza inquired. Tallah laughed, "I would take Luna if Kenai wouldn't rip my head off. I'll probably end up going alone. Again. Or I might ask Cadence. She wants me." Victor snorted, and Tallah raised an eyebrow, "You think that's funny, tough boy? Who are you taking?" Victor looked to the ground, embarrassed. "Oh, well, I, um...my cousin. My dad's making me take my cousin who's coming to visit." Tallah raised an eyebrow, "Uh-huh. Right. What about you, Rosebud?" Roza shrugged, "I'll go alone. I hate parties anyway." Tallah feigned a heart attack, "How can you hate parties? The dancing, the music, the lights!" Victor gave him a look, "You're thinking of human parties." Tallah came out of his reverie, "Oh, yeah."

"Okay, guys. So what's today's plan?" Victor and Tallah looked at each other. Tallah smiled, "Why don't you transform into a human and strike up some convo with Prince Martin?" Roza looked at him, her mouth agape, "Martin? Transform into a human and talk to Martin? Are you insane? That's forbidden!" Victor shrugged, "What have you cared before? Besides, he's been wondering about his mystery girl for a year. Maybe he should get some sort of reward for being so faithful." Tallah laughed, "Besides, we need information for the raid. We need to figure out what their arsenal's like, and what's a better way than gaining their trust and just asking?" Roza looked to the ground, "I don't know, guys. I'm not that great at lying…" Victor swatted her playfully in the arm, "That's the point. You don't have to lie. Just be you! Trust us."

"Okay, kid, there you go." Tallah pushed Roza forward and she transformed into a human, "Now just go inconspicuously capture his attention. You can do it!" he called as Roza walked nervously towards the village. Tallah became serious and turned towards Victor, "Do you think it'll work?" he whispered. Victor narrowed his eyes, "It has to."

Roza tried to calm herself down. *Be calm, act cool,* she thought to herself, *it's not a big deal. Pretend like you belong.* That had been Tallah's first word of advice when he started teaching her to be a wolf. Roza took a deep breath and walked calmly up to the stables that she knew Martin and Justin played by. She stuck her hand out to one of the horses, a beautiful palomino, who nuzzled her hand and continued to search her body for any signs of food. Roza laughed, "I have nothing for you!" she cried as the horse's nose tickled her.

"It's you!" she heard from behind her. Abruptly, she turned around to see a wide-eyed Martin and disbelieving Justin. She froze. What did she do now? Her first instinct was to run, so she did.

"Wait!" cried Martin, running after her. She was fast, faster than anybody he'd ever come across, "Wait!" Roza looked over her shoulder and saw Martin holding his knees, panting, and she slowed down to a jog and hid in the shadows of some bushes. Martin caught his breath and stood up, "Where did she go?" he asked his brother, who had just caught up. Justin pointed in her general direction, "Somewhere over there, I think. Martin, are you sure this is a good—" but Martin was already calling out to her, "Come back! I won't hurt you, I promise! Who are you?" Roza watched from the bushes as his face became increasingly forlorn, and decided to do it. She couldn't have Tallah and Victor calling her a chicken. She stood up and stepped out from the bushes, hiding partially behind a tree.

Martin caught her eyes, those rich green eyes that sparkled with golden specks. He stepped towards her cautiously, but she didn't even move. He walked closer and said in a calm voice, "I'm Martin, and this is my brother, Justin. Who are you?" and he heard a small voice as clear as bells, "Roza." Martin sighed. Roza. What a beautiful name. He stuck out his hand, "Won't you come with us, Roza?" Roza stepped out from behind the tree, but did not take his hand. They led her to the area where they often played and sat down.

"Where did you come from?" asked Justin. Roza looked to the ground, "Lodos." the boys' eyes widened, "Lodos?" they asked at the same time, and Martin continued, "What on earth are you doing here? You could be killed!" Roza looked at him with a puzzled gaze, and Justin explained, "The king, my father, has just put in a new law that all citizens of Lodos are considered traitors to the crown. He's quite paranoid." Martin nodded, "You could be killed just for being here. You must leave!" Roza shook her head, "I can't." Justin gave her a look, "Why not?" Roza played with a blade of grass, "I live here."

"Where?" questioned Martin. Roza replied, "In the woods." Justin and Martin looked at one another again, "The woods?" Justin exclaimed, "What on earth are you doing there?" Roza realized what she had said, and became nervous, "I, um, I just, uh..." Justin's gaze saddened, "You live on your own." Roza shook her head, "No, no, no! I don't live on my own, I um, live with my friends." Martin was bewildered, "Your friends? There's a whole group of you living in the woods?" Roza nodded, "Yes." Martin stood up, "We must find them, this is not right!" Roza stood up with him, "No! I mean, they're fine. I mean, they're not kids like me. They're animals." Martin almost laughed, "Animals?" while Justin was serious, "You live with wild animals? Are you mad?" Roza became defensive, "They're my friends, and my family. Of course I live with them." Justin shook his head, "It is not proper for you to be living in such conditions. Don't you have parents?"

Roza didn't know what to do. If these two, apparently the princes of this country, found out that she was the princess of a country they hated and considered traitorous, what would they do? Would they turn her in? Well…she didn't have to mention the fact that she was a princess. She could just tell them the truth.

"My parents died when I was a baby." Martin and Justin looked at each other, "Then you must come with us! We shall find you proper clothing and food and a place to stay rather than the filthy woods." Martin seemed quite excited about this idea, but Justin looked unsure. Was that really such a wise idea, to bring a complete stranger into their home? Before he had the chance to say anything, Roza spoke up, "No. Thank you. But I really mustn't. I should go."

Martin panicked. This may be his only chance to see this girl again. "Wait!" he cried, and then he tried to come up with an excuse for her to stay, "Would you, um...would you like to see the horses?" Roza wasn't sure what to say, but when she saw Victor and Tallah nodding vigorously, she agreed, "Of course." Martin smiled, relieved, "Justin, if you would, um, leave us alone?" Justin caught his drift, and walked away with an exasperated expression on his face. Martin smiled and took Roza's hand, "Shall we?" and he walked most princely towards the stables. Roza recognized the palomino horse she'd befriended earlier and laughed as she was searched for food again.

"That's Marisol. She's a sweetheart." Roza let out a small chuckle, "Hungry, I suppose." Martin raised an eyebrow to her and cleared his throat, "Um, this might be a little sudden, but would you come to the Summer Solstice Ball with me in two days?" Roza's eyes widened, "A ball?" Martin nodded, "They're dreadfully boring. I'm sure you would make them much more interesting. At least I'd have someone to converse with. Come on, you'll love it!" Roza sighed, "I don't know...I mean..." and she thought about it. A boy was asking her to a ball, an interesting boy at that. Who was she to turn a prince down?

"I'd love to." she gave him a smile, and with a small curtsy, she ran off.

Roza ducked behind a tree and breathed in and out deeply, and then she returned to her wolf form. She ran to meet Victor and Tallah, who were pacing and mumbling behind a patch of bushes. Victor looked up, "What took you so long? What happened?" Tallah joined him and grinned, "Yeah, how did it go?" Roza smiled, "I got invited to a ball! We're in!" Victor rolled his eyes, but Tallah gasped, "A ball? A real ball? Rosebud, you're so lucky! I'm so super jealous of you!" Victor snorted, "Yeah, okay, great. So when is this ball?" Roza sighed, "Two days."

—

"Now remember, head up, shoulders back, stomach in, polite smile! Don't slouch! Good. You'll do great tonight!" Roza was becoming increasingly annoyed with Tallah's orders, but knew it was for the best. She couldn't just go to a ball and act like a commoner, she was a royal, and for once, she needed to act like one. Victor, who was on the ground with his eyes closed and his arms behind his head, snorted, "Tallah, you've been coaching her for days. She's fine. Now we just need to worry about one thing." Roza gave him a look, "And what is that, O Wise One?" Victor stood up and laughed, "Um, a *dress*, maybe? What, you're going to go in rags? Great fashion choice, Cinderella." Tallah scoffed, "And what do you know about fashion, Tough Guy?" Victor rolled his eyes, "Whatever. All I know is that girls wear dresses, and she doesn't have one that's good enough." Roza turned to Tallah, "Victor's right. I can't just show up in my everyday clothes." Tallah sighed and rolled his eyes, "It was *supposed* to be a surprise, Victor, you no-good ingrate, but fine. Wait here." Tallah left Victor and Roza, muttering to himself as he walked away.

Victor looked at Roza and cleared his throat, "I, um, I hope you do well tonight." Roza nodded, "Yeah, um, I think I'll be fine. Just ask about the weapons and battle tactics and stuff, right?" Victor nodded, "Right. Pretty straightforward." Roza nodded again, "Uh-huh. And um, you know that they know I'm from Lodos, right? I mean, it's totally not weird to have a girl from Lodos asking about Alacrast's battle tactics and weaponry." Victor slapped his forehead, "Oh, my god. You told them? Now what? Why didn't you tell us before?" Roza shrugged, "It slipped my mind. Now what do we do?" Victor paced back and forth, completely unsure. What would they do? Would they throw her in the dungeon? Have her tried for treason? Kill her on the spot? No, they wouldn't do that, it would look bad.

Tallah came back, parcel in hand, "We may not be completely human, but that doesn't mean that we don't have skills when it comes to clothing." He unwrapped the brown package and let Victor and Roza gaze at it. It was a pink gown made of gossamer-like material. Its sleeves were short and flowy, the waist bound with a thin white ribbon. Tallah blushed, "I know it's not much, but it's simple. I thought you'd like it. Except for the pink. Sorry for the pink. I like pink." Roza laughed, "Tallah, it's beautiful! You made this? You're amazing! Thank you!" she took the dress and left to change.

Victor turned to Tallah, "Okay, Dressmaker, you've got to find us some stuff." Tallah gave him a look, "Stuff? Do you mean—" Victor swatted him, "No! Not that. Some clothes, whatever black things that the boys wear to fancy stuff." Tallah rolled his eyes, "It wouldn't kill you to learn what a tuxedo or suit is..." Victor glared, "Yes, yes I think it would. Seriously, though. We're going." Tallah gave him a skeptic look, "Going? Going where?" Victor tousled his hair, "To the party, of course. We'll attend the party with Their Highnesses and then have some fun, and perhaps a, um...tour." Tallah put his hands on his hips, "Tour? You mean sneaking around." Victor shrugged, "Well, if you'd rather put it that way. Now just get us some suits and I'm going to take a bath." Tallah feigned a heart attack, "A...bath? Like, a real bath? Oh, Victor, is it that bad? You didn't tell me you were going to die so soon!" Victor rolled his eyes, "Idiot."

"So...does it look okay?" Roza came out of the bushes. Her hair was no longer tied back, instead it rolled down her back in gentle waves. The pink dress flowed from her midsection out in an A-line. Tallah squealed, "Rosebud, you look beautiful! Brava to me!" Victor ran his fingers through his hair and said nothing. Roza looked at him uncertainly, "Is something wrong?" Victor shook his head slowly, "No, it's…you're…" Tallah rolled his eyes, "Okay, Rosebud, um, would you give us a moment?" Roza nodded and went off to think by the lake.

Tallah led Victor away, "You are so obvious!" Victor looked at him, insulted, "Oblivious?" Tallah shook his head, "No. Obvious. As in it's obvious you like her!" Victor snorted, "I have to if I don't want her to rip my head off." Tallah rolled his eyes and brought his hands to his face, "No, you idiot. You like her, as in like her! Like this!" he made kissing noises towards Victor, who shrunk away. "Eww, stop that! I do not like her!" Tallah laughed, "That, my friend, is a dirty lie. Come on, she was beautiful. Even your cold heart can't turn away from that. She's a princess, after all. They tend to capture the heart." Victor's eyes widened, "Princess?" Tallah nodded, "She never told you? Yes, her parents are the king and queen of Lodos, so going to that party puts her in a lot of danger if she's found out." Victor looked over to Roza, who was playing with a shy rabbit, "We're putting her in danger? And you knew? How could you! What if she gets hurt? What happens then? It'll be our fault!"

Tallah clapped Victor on the back, "She can take care of herself. She'll be alright. Besides, they won't find out as long as we don't bring it up." Tallah sighed and walked to the edge of a lake, motioning for Victor to follow him. Victor snarled, "A lake? You brought us to a lake to get fancy clothes?" Tallah sighed, "Suits, Vic, suits. And no, we have to travel to the island." Victor got in the tiny boat, hidden by branches and shrubbery, and grabbed an oar, "Island? What island?" Tallah shrugged, "Don't know what it's called. I was wandering around one day and saw it in the distance, so I found this little thing and went to investigate. Nobody's there; it's completely deserted, but you can still see the remnants of where natives used to live, and there's a castle." Victor didn't know that rowing was this hard of work. His shoulders and arms ached, his lungs begged for air. "What do you mean, a castle?" Apparently, Tallah was quite used to this, as he had no trouble at all. "It's some old, abandoned castle. Left completely intact, with clothing, food, silverware, weapons, everything. All it needs is a little dusting and some light. Maybe some fire in the fireplace to warm it up and it's as good as new. It can't have been abandoned for long." Victor was curious now, "Come on, let's get to this castle. Somehow, you've got me interested."

As they pulled the boat to shore, an uneasy feeling settled among the both of them, and Tallah chuckled nervously, "Did I tell you that it's also kind of creepy?" Victor sighed, "Figured that one out myself. Come on, is that it?" he pointed to a dark, run-down castle that was engulfed by vines.

Tallah began to climb up the steps of the old, ruined castle that once must have been grand. Victor followed him quickly up the stairs into a bedroom, "What is this place?" Tallah shrugged as he rifled through a closet, "Like I said, some old castle. Why are there only baby clothes in here? Ugh, next." They went into a room that was slightly bigger, with no bed, only baskets of fabric and needles and thread and comfy chairs. Tallah opened the drawers of the dresser in the corner, "Aha! Here, these should fit just fine." He tossed a pair of black pants, a red band, a white buttoned-down shirt, a weird red ribbon thing, and a coat to him. "Go!" he commanded, "Try them on. Shirt first, pants second, red band third, bow tie fourth, and the coat goes on last. Oh, here's some gloves! Your hands are probably dirty." Victor gave a secret snarl to him, but did as he wished.

Victor began to dress, eventually messing with the bow tie. What were these things? Why were they so hard to tie? What was the purpose of it? But once he looked at Tallah, with a white bow tie and waistband, he understood that it was supposed to look like a girl's bow. Tallah finally noticed him and laughed, "Can't get it tied? Here." he came over and somehow (presumably by magic, Victor mused) it was tied. "Now come on, put this cloak on so you don't get dirty, and let's go meet the beautiful princess."

Roza paced back and forth at the edge of the forest. She'd brushed her hair twice and had washed it and made sure it wasn't hanging in her face too much. She'd tried to put some color in her skin but the only thing she could seem to manage to do was burn or blush, and both were unattractive. For the fourth time, she smelled her breath. Decent enough, didn't smell like anything in particular. Ugh, where were those boys? They were going to be late!

"Miss us?" Tallah called from afar. Roza gasped in amazement, "You guys, you're...you're clean! And dressed nicely! Tallah! What did you do to Victor?" Tallah laughed, "I gave him a bath. Now come on, let's go." and with a boy at either arm, they made their way to the castle gate, where they were greeted and let in.

"This is amazing!" Tallah exclaimed, and Roza rolled her eyes, "It's alright. It's just a party. They're kind of boring, if you ask me." Tallah snorted, "In that case, I'm not asking you. Hors d'oeuvres, here I come!" but Victor grabbed him, "We're supposed to be her escorts, not the food tasters. That boy and his brother are waving to us. Come on." Roza broke free of the boys and went to meet Martin.

"Roza, you look beautiful! Who are these?" Roza curtsied slightly, "Thank you. These are Tallah, and Victor, my, eh...brothers." Victor tried to keep his cool. He didn't like the look of this Martin boy. He was too posh, too proper, too...something. Martin smiled politely, "Pleased to meet you. I am Martin, and this is my brother, Justin. We're very glad to have you here. Roza didn't mention she had brothers." Tallah cleared his throat, "Victor, perhaps if you would like to take Roza to the hors d'oeuvres table for a drink? She looks quite parched." Victor nodded, "Come on, Ro." they bowed and curtsied slightly to the princes and left Tallah to work his magic.

Victor poured them each a cup of a sparkling drink, "A princess, hmm?" Roza almost choked, "Excuse me?" Victor turned his gaze away from her, "Tallah said you were a princess. Is it true?" Roza sighed, "I didn't mean to not tell you or anything, but it was never important. Besides, if you'd have known, you never would have let it go." Victor smirked, "Never important? It was always important! I never would have done those terrible things to you at the beginning had I known. I never would have let you converse with your rival country's princes! I never would have put you in danger. You're too important." Roza raised an eyebrow, "Important?" Victor cleared his throat, "Important to the pack, that is. And your kingdom." Roza shook her head, "Nobody is going to want me for a leader." Victor frowned, "Why not? With your, erm, charm and quick wit, I'm sure you'd make a fair queen. A little on the tough side, maybe, but hey, it builds character."

Roza didn't reply. She was off in the distance, in her own world. Victor looked to Tallah, who was laughing with the princes, and took Roza's hand, "Ro, I'm sorry. I just…I don't want anything to happen to you. You're my best friend." Roza sighed and nodded, "I know. But I can take care of myself. I'm not helpless." Victor smiled and looked at the ground, and then into her eyes, "Trust me, I know." Tallah caught his gaze and nodded slightly, motioning them over.

"Come on, Ro, let's go." Roza gladly put down her drink and let Victor lead her to Tallah, Martin, and Justin, who were all jesting and laughing. Victor cleared his throat, "We are rather sorry, Your Highnesses, but we must be going. It is quite past young Roza's bedtime!" Roza looked to Victor, enraged, but when she saw the urgency in his eyes, she played along. "Oh, yes!" she yawned and stretched, "I am simply exhausted. The party was wonderful, thank you for inviting me. Good night!" she curtsied slightly, and they sped out of the castle as quickly as they could. They ran and transformed into their wolf forms.

Victor looked to the sky, which bore a full moon, "We need to get the information to Dire right now. The raid will start soon." Tallah nodded, "We have to hurry! If they start without us, we could be caught in the middle of it. We need to reach the pack." Roza pointed her head to the left, "Come on. I know a shortcut."

By the time they reached the pack, they were out of breath. Dire was furious, "You insolent pups, where were you?" Victor went to him, "Sir, we have gotten the information you requested. Tallah must have conference with you." Dire sighed, "Very well. Come along, Tallah. The rest of you, get ready." Luna and Kenai glared at Roza, "Where were you? Off being a princess?" Roza was confused, "What?" Kenai glared at her, "Dire spilled it all to us tonight, that we had to keep you safe or else because you're one of the princesses of Lodos." Luna stuck up her nose, "Now you're special? What next, these two are princes? I'm looking out for myself and my sister, and that's it. I don't need to take care of some snobby, stuck-up princess!" Victor growled, "She's not snobby or stuck up! And you will worry about her or else you'll answer to me!" by this time he was up close and personal with both wolves, and very, very angry, "Understand?" both wolves nodded sheepishly and scampered off. Roza was surprised.

"Victor, you didn't have to do that. It's okay, I'm used to much worse insults. They were just angry and worried." Victor gave her a sad glance, "You shouldn't have to be used to those kind of comments, Ro. You're one of the most kind-hearted people I've ever known, despite your somewhat rough exterior. Please, at least let me guard you." Roza shook her head, "I can't, Victor. I can take care of myself. You taught me how to fight, weapons or no. I can do this. You just look out for yourself and Tallah, okay?" Victor sighed and was about to speak when there was a howl from Dire, who had returned with Tallah.

"Plans of attack have not changed. Their arsenal is small. They don't have many guards on duty tonight, but do not take this lightly. This is the most important mission of your life. I expect to be triumphant. To your places." All of the wolves scattered to their different groups. Roza was with Tallah, Victor, Luna, and Kenai.

"Come on, we're last. Ears up, listen for the signal." Victor whispered. Everyone nodded and crouched down low, waiting.

"How could she just leave like that, Justin? *Bedtime*?" Justin shrugged, "Perhaps she doesn't really like parties. Remember, she does live in the woods. Maybe it's best if you forget and leave her alone." Martin was about to say something when they heard a scream. Everyone looked to the source of the scream and joined in as they saw five wolves at the door to the ballroom.

"Children, come along!" their mother ushered Martin, Justin, and their little sister Anna out of the ballroom and into the servant's quarters, where she grabbed a parcel and fled through the cellar door.

"Mother, where are we going?" Martin cried. His mother looked back with a sad, worried look on her face, and stopped them by the stables. "Here, Rhian! Come on now!" she grabbed Martin and Anna and put them on the enormous black Friesian. She went to take hold of Justin, but he was not there. "Justin!" she cried, "Justin, where are you?" but he was nowhere to be found. With tears streaming down her face, she looked at Martin. "Here," she said, handing him the parcel, "Take this. Use your father's sword if you must. The rest is for Anna, to remember us by. Get to Lodos, it's the only place that's safe. I love you." and without another word, she commanded the horse forward, and ran. Martin tried to stop the horse, but Rhian was too scared. "Mother!" he cried, "Mother!" but she was gone.

Martin wiped the tears from his eyes and looked ahead. There was a port nearby where they could escape into Lodos on a ship. With a determined mind, he ushered the horse forward, but Rhian would not go. He had stopped on the top of a flat hill, his ears back, and eyes wide. "What's wrong, Rhian?" Martin asked, but his question was answered sooner than later as several pairs of yellow eyes appeared out of the darkness. Martin hopped down from the horse and grabbed his father's sword, prepared to fight. To his surprise, though, the wolves did not attack. The eyes seemed to make a path, and out of seemingly nowhere came a pair of rich green eyes. It was a young wolf, smaller than the others, whose gaze was locked with his.

The wolf growled and attempted to pounce on him, but Martin dodged and swung the heavy sword, which missed the wolf by a great distance. Barking, the wolf leapt at him again, swinging its paws around madly. Martin brought the sword up above his head and slammed it down straight into the wolf's shoulder. The wolf cried out and two of the others jumped ahead and growled viciously. The bigger wolf had angry eyes, and Martin could tell he was ready to attack when all of a sudden there was a haunting howl from off in the distance. Everything became calm, and the bigger wolf picked up the injured one, carried it on its back, and went on their way.

Martin was breathing heavily, but put the sword in the sheath on the horse's saddle and climbed back up, where Anna had buried her face in his mane. With a swing of the reins, they cantered forward. With one glance back, he saw a large, mangled, disfigured wolf with eyes as red as blood on the roof of the castle, the town in flames. This time, though, he didn't cry.

"Roza! Roza, come on, talk to me!" Victor set her down and transformed into his human form as she involuntarily had after the attack. Her eyes were closed in pain, and small groans were coming from her unmoving mouth. Her left shoulder was torn and wouldn't stop bleeding, so Tallah brought over leaves to put pressure on the wound. Victor looked to Luna and Kenai, "This is why we look out for each other, not ourselves! Understand? Now go and fetch Dire and the Healer." with guilty looks on their faces, they obeyed.

Tallah looked to Victor worriedly, "Is she going to be okay?" Victor shook his head, "I don't know, just apply as much pressure as possible. I'll keep her as conscious as I can." Tallah nodded, and Victor sighed and touched her face, "Ro, Ro, come on, don't do this to me. I'm right here,

Tallah's right here, you can't go now. Don't you want to shoot some arrows tomorrow or chase the rabbits? I'll even swim if you want me to!" but she didn't stir.

"What's all this?" it was Dire. Victor moved slightly, "Sir, she was attacked by the prince. His sword sliced her shoulder." Dire called the Healer over, "Nukta, what do you say?" Nukta motioned for Tallah to move and removed the leaves, examining the wounds, "She must go home." she said in an old, dry voice. "I do not have the knowledge to heal this wound. Her family will. She must go immediately." Victor nodded, "We'll take her." but Nukta shook her head, "You don't belong there. Dire, take her home. We will be waiting for you." Dire nodded, transformed into a human, and picked her up. Victor stood, enraged, "No! We're her best friends, we have to go! I'm not leaving her." Dire shoved him aside with his shoulder, "You have no choice, boy. Now move over." Victor and Tallah both pounded on his back, "No!" they cried, "Let us go, you have to let us go! We're not leaving her!" but Nukta held them both back with surprising strength, "No. You will stay here." Tallah sniffled, "Will she be back?" Nukta sighed, "I do not think so, Grandson. She has learned what she can, now she must go back. She is a human, not a wolf."

Victor broke free of her grasp and ran after Dire, but he was nowhere to be found. Without a word, he sunk to the ground, and began to cry.

CHAPTER 2:

"Ana, do I have to go?" Roza was sitting on Ana's lap, letting her hair be brushed. Ana sighed, "Of course! It's your sisters' birthdays. I know you don't want to go, but it'll be different this time. Maybe you'll be invited to dance." Roza laughed, "Ha. Dance. Everyone's afraid of me, Ana. No one will want to dance with me." Ana stopped brushing and put the comb on the vanity. She turned Roza's face towards herself and cupped her cheek, "People are only afraid of what they don't understand. And they don't understand that you are my special, sweet girl whom I love very much." Roza accepted her hug, but did not smile. "They make fun of me, and talk behind my back."

Ana looked at her worriedly, "Who makes fun of you?" Roza sighed, "Not others, just Cordelia, Raya, Russ, Sasha, Hope, Mel, Ember, and Coda." those were Ana and Garren's seven girls and young boy. They also had another son, Kendall, who was married and ruled his own kingdom. Ana shook her head, "Like I said, they don't understand. And they're your siblings, of course they'll make fun of you. You make fun of them. They don't mean anything by it. Now where's your dress?" Roza stuck out her tongue, "That hideous thing is in the closet. Can't I just wear a normal one?" Ana gave her a stern look, "Miss Roza Kiara Collins, you will wear what I say you will wear. You are a princess of this country and will be presented as one." When Roza folded her arms across her chest and looked away, Ana softened her gaze, "I know you hate them, but we must present ourselves as best as possible. It's the duty and life of a princess. We have no choice. Besides, it's only for a few hours."

"Why can't it be like the Blue Moon Feast?" Roza growled under her breath, "I miss the wolves. It's been a year! I want to go back." Ana grabbed the dress and shook her head, "You're human, Roza, not a wolf. That's simply a power that comes with being you. You'll see your friends again, but for right now, Dire has forbidden it." Roza rolled her eyes, "Why do we have to do what Dire says? I'll bet if we all teamed together, Victor, Tallah and I could beat him in two seconds!" Ana tied the silk sash around the red dress, "I'm sure. That's my brave little girl. Now come on, put on your shoes and tiara and let's go downstairs. People are probably wondering where we are."

Roza sat at a glass and gold table far back in the corner of the ballroom, listening to the music and drawing designs with her finger on the table's surface. A little girl, almost identical to Roza, and also a ward of the royal family, sat next to her prim and properly. Roza looked at her and rolled her eyes, "You look like a dog waiting for a biscuit, Anya." Anya scoffed at her, "And you look like a slob. Your hair is barely brushed." Roza shrugged, "No one is going to talk to me, anyway. What's the point?" Anya shrugged, "Whatever you say. Now, who do you think Russ is going to end up with tonight?"

Roza snorted, "Who knows? But, hey, who's that?" she looked at a young boy with brown hair and a green suit who was coming up to Anya quite nervously. He cleared his throat as his voice shook, "Miss Anastasia, may I have this dance, please?" Anya looked at Roza, who nodded, trying to stifle a laugh. Anya glared at her and stood, extending her hand into his, "Of course."

They went off to the dance floor and left Roza to roll her eyes and sulk. Without Anya, now what was she to do? She saw the way people looked at her with fear and hate in their eyes. They would whisper as she walked by, they stood back as she got closer. They'd always acted like this. At least nothing had changed in the time she'd been gone.

"Um…Are you Roza?" Roza looked up from her daydream in surprise. Standing in front of her was a blonde-haired, blue-eyed, handsome young boy with a royal blue and gold suit. He appeared slightly nervous. Roza nodded, "Yes. Who are you?" The boy bowed slightly, "James Delarosa, miss. Would you care to dance?" Roza's jaw dropped, "Um…uh…yeah. I mean, yes. Thank you."

Roza took James' hand and let herself be led to the dance floor. He took her waist, pulled her close, and spun. Roza cocked her head to the side, "Pardon my manners, but have we met before? You seem quite familiar." James quickly shook his head, "I could never forget a girl like you." Roza blushed and gave a small smile, "Thank you for the compliment." James laughed, "Of course. You're quite pretty, you know, even for being a Faelis." Roza stopped dancing, "What?" James was confused, "What? Did I say something wrong?" Roza noticed how he looked to two other boys, one much older and one closer in age, who were snickering. She fumed, "I am just feeling a bit dizzy. If you'll excuse me."

Roza balled her fists and slumped down in her chair. She should have known he was made to dance with her. No one in their right mind would honestly say that about her. Pretty for a Faelis. What a fool she was.

Anya came back to the table, dazed and confused. Roza sat up, "What's wrong?" Anya shook her head, "I think he liked me. He actually liked me. Who on earth would like me?" Roza laughed, "Anya, you're the smartest person I know, not to mention you're really pretty. Of course the right guy would like you. They're idiots not to look past your icy barrier."

"I suppose, but—" Anya silenced as the candles lighting the room all suddenly went out. Roza grabbed her sister's hand as a few select candles returned to life with a blue flame. There was a shadow of a young man with blades at his side leaping from the balcony, attacking someone.

"Ana!" Roza cried as she saw the queen fall to the floor. She leapt up, but was blocked by the crowd screaming and panicking. Anya looked at her in fear, and Roza caught the eye of Kendall trying to get her attention. "Run!" he cried, taking her shoulders. "Roza, you have to run. Run away. Take Anya. Don't come back!" Roza shook her head furiously, "What? No, Kendall, what do you mean?" Kendall pushed her away, "They're after you! They'll want Anya next! Go! Now!" Roza was horrified, but she grabbed her sister's hand and dragged Anya in the opposite direction of the crowd, down the stairwell into the servants' quarters and out the back side of the castle, where the woods lie.

"Roza!" Anya cried, but Roza pulled her along, running as fast as she could without turning into a wolf. They stopped after almost a mile of running to catch their breaths. Roza looked at her dress, which was in ruins, and started to tear it apart. Anya spoke in between breaths, "What…are…you doing?" Roza didn't look up as she commented, "All these petticoats will slow us down. Rip yours off." Anya didn't question her, she simply nodded and did the same.

"What are we doing?" she asked when she was done. Roza sighed, "Kendall told us to run. I've never seen him so scared or desperate. That man attacked Ana, which means he was probably after the whole family. He was an assassin. We're running away," she grabbed Anya's hand and looked at her, "and we're not coming back."

—

"I'll trade you this cat-eye for your shooter." Violet looked at Lily with a disgusted look, "No way! Three cat's-eyes for the shooter. And a penny." Lily stood up and sat on her rusty bed. It creaked beneath her weight. "I don't have a penny! And neither do you!" Roza rolled her eyes, "No one here has a penny, you two. Nobody except for Mr. Worthington." they looked at her and stuck out their tongues, "Shut up, you no-name! You don't know anything! You and your sister are so dumb!" Lily nodded, "Yeah, you should just go back to where you came from!" Roza stood up, "Shut up or I'll punch you again. And this time I won't go easy." Violet stepped in front of Lily, "Mr. Worthington said he'll send you off on the orphan train if you caused any more trouble. Without your dumb sister."

Roza narrowed her eyes, "Please. Nobody could send me anywhere without my sister." Violet and Lily looked at each other and snickered, "Yeah, well, say that when you see Annie on the train tomorrow." Roza stepped closer to them, "It's Anya. And what do you mean? They wouldn't send her off. She's too young." Violet shrugged, "Mr. Worthington thought you'd behave better and be able to be adopted and out of here quicker if you didn't have a reason to fight so much." Roza almost slapped her, but realized that Violet wasn't the one she was angry at. They were going to send Anya on the orphan train? She had to get her and get out of there before they put her on that train. She wasn't old enough to go work somewhere, and she wouldn't know how to get back to her. Roza shoved Lily and Violet down onto Lily's bed and went running out of the older girls' dormitory. Anya was in the younger girls' dormitory, across the vast building. Now she just had to get over there without being seen. *You can do this. Slow and steady. Silent. Stealthy.*

Roza started slinking slowly and silently across the walkway balcony over the entrance to the orphanage. She made it across with no problem, but the tricky part was going to be getting past all of the volunteer maids that were almost worse than Mr. Worthington. She breathed in and out silently, calming herself, and started to sneak against the walls slowly and silently towards the dormitory. Roza could do this at night without a problem; there was never anybody in these halls at night. It was a completely different experience in bright daylight. She knew anybody could see her in her faded brown dress against the stark white walls. She just had to get past the office, where Mr. Worthington worked most of the day, brushing his mustache and putting oils on his dry, sandpaper hands. Roza climbed onto the railing that topped the winding stairs, and crawled along it very slowly, so he couldn't hear her footsteps. She made the mistake of looking down and suddenly became very afraid. Roza hated heights. What if she fell? She would die, surely. Then nobody could take care of Anya. She'd be left all alone. Who knew what would happen to her?

Get a grip! Roza snapped out of her fear, and slowly made her way to the end of the hall. She climbed off of the railing and gave a sigh of relief. Now she just had to go into the dormitory, grab Anya, and get out of there as quick as possible. No more orphanages for them!

Roza made her way towards the door and had her hand on the doorknob when she felt a hand on her shoulder. It was rough and calloused, and it gripped tight. She froze.

"Lost, are we?" spoke a rough, gravelly voice, like the hands it bore. Roza said nothing. He chuckled, "I didn't think so. Come with me. Now." He took her into his office and shoved her into a chair. "What do you think you're doing near this dormitory?" Roza stood up, "You can't send Anya on the orphan train! It's illegal to separate families!" Mr. Worthington pushed her down again. "Don't yell at me, girl. I can do anything I want with her. She's going on that train. She's young and will learn quickly. She'll go fast. As for you, I've got to make sure you learn your place." Roza narrowed her eyes, "I'm not doing anything you want if she goes on that train." he looked at her with contempt, but said nothing.

Later that night, Roza couldn't sleep. She'd been formulating plan after plan of how she was going to get Anya and herself out of there tonight. They had to leave. She hated this place anyway. They hadn't meant to be caught.

"You! Girls! What do you think you're doing?" Roza looked over, shocked. A man in a police shirt was coming quickly towards them. She grabbed Anya's hand and the bottle of milk they'd been grabbing and ran as fast as she could. Anya was having trouble keeping up. "Come on, Anya! Faster!" but she couldn't run faster, and she tripped, pulling Roza down with her. The bottle broke,

and milk spilled everywhere. The cop caught up with them, "Who are you girls? Where are your parents?" Roza was breathing heavily, "We have none." Anya looked at her and tried to protest, but Roza gave her a cutting look, "We have no family." The cop cleared his throat, "Then you're going to have to come with me."

Roza thought he'd take them somewhere with hot food and warm beds, but instead he brought them to this dirty orphanage where no one was allowed to speak, no one was allowed to laugh, no one was allowed to do anything. It was her mistake for trusting him.

Someone touched her arm. Roza bolted up, grabbed the arm and twisted. She heard a whimper, "Let go! Let go!" a voice whispered urgently. Roza let go, "Anya?" she asked tentatively. The dark figure nodded and they embraced, "Anya! Oh, Anya, you're going on the train tomorrow. We have to get out of here." Anya nodded, "I know. Jitter told me." Jitter was a quiet girl in Roza's dormitory who was always being bullied for being small and handicapped. Roza looked next to Anya and saw another figure with crutches. "Thanks," she whispered, "now let's get out of here."

They crept out of the dormitory and to the stairs that led to the main floor. Roza, Anya, and Jitter managed to make it to the landing without too much trouble, and when they reached the back door, Anya turned around and hugged Jitter, "Thank you. We'll come back for you and get you out before they send you away, too." Jitter smiled, "Don't worry about me. No one wants a cripple for a maid or daughter, so I'm not going anywhere. Just get out of here." Roza grabbed Anya's hand. "Thanks, Jitter. Let's go, Anya." and without another word, they opened the door, and bolted.

"No more orphanages, Anya! We can't trust them. From now on, we take care of ourselves, got it?" Anya tried to keep up, "Got it." they came to a bridge, and crawled underneath. Roza was thankful it had been dry and hot lately. She laid down next to Anya. Anya sighed, "I don't understand. Why can't we go back home?" Roza sighed, "Kendall told us not to. He said we had to stay away no matter what, and never come back. There was a reason. Kendall is wise. We have to do what he says." Anya took her sister's hand, "But Roza, will we *ever* go back?" Roza sighed, shook her head, and laid on her back, "I don't know, Anya. I really don't. All I know is that we have to keep going, but we can't be noticed. We're street kids now. Cops will be looking for us, wanting to take us to orphanages and jails. We can't trust them. We can't trust anyone. And we have to do something about these orphanages. Tomorrow, I start teaching you how to fight, like Victor taught me." Anya turned to face her sister and closed her eyes, "Tell me about Victor and Tallah again." and so she did.

CHAPTER 3:

"Matthias! Matthias!" Justin rushed his brother into the large castle that belonged to their older cousin, Matthias. Martin was shivering and confused, "Martin," Justin sat him down on a plush chaise lounge in the middle of a large and luxurious sitting room, "I can't believe I found you! What happened?" Martin opened his mouth and made a few sounds, but no words came out. Justin sighed, "Come, brother, we speak in the morning." and he ushered him off to bed.

A very large, muscular man put his hand on Justin's shoulder as he shut the door to the room Martin was sleeping in. "Is he alright?" he asked in a deep, husky voice that was tinted with concern. Justin shook his head, "I'm not sure, Matthias. I don't know what's wrong with him. Shock, probably. If he isn't better in the morning, I'll send for the doctor, but for now…all we can do is wait." Matthias nodded, "Let us get some rest, then. I have a feeling that tomorrow may be taxing if he is not well." Justin smiled a little, "Good idea. Good night." and he went off to his room.

"Justin! Justin!" Justin awoke to being shaken and his name being shouted. He opened his eyes to see a panicked Martin, and bolted awake. "Martin, what's wrong? Are you alright? What happened?" Martin hugged his brother, "Justin, I've been looking for you everywhere! How did you get here? How did I get here?" Justin chuckled, "Let's go find Matthias and something to eat, we'll talk about it then."

"Well, look who's awake! Took you two long enough." Matthias boomed as they entered the grand dining room. The servants served them juice and tea on a silver tray with coffee, cream, and sugar. There were yeast rolls with fresh butter, buttermilk and oats, fruit, and jam with bread. Martin took a serving of each, and Matthias laughed, "Hungry, are we? I don't blame you. How long had you been out there? What happened?" Martin shook his head, "I'm not sure. I remember Mother putting Anna and I on the horse, we went to the dock and convinced a captain of a ship to allow us passage to Lodos, and there was a fight one night. One of the drunk men tried to take Anna, mistaking her for his daughter...after that, nothing. Until last night, everything is just...gone." Justin looked up from his plate in alarm, "Anna? What happened to her? Where is she?" Martin couldn't look them in the eyes as he shook his head, "I don't know." Justin looked at Matthias, "We must find her. She's just a small child, she'll never survive on her own!"

Matthias put down his silverware and stood up, "I agree. I shall contact the police force at once. Justin, if you would?" Justin nodded and stood up to follow him. Martin slammed his fist down onto the table, "He is only a year older! You can't expect me to do nothing!" Matthias and Justin looked to each other, "Very well," Matthias eventually decided, "you're a smart young lad. Come with us, then. Don't cause any trouble, though. We need to be patient. That is the key." Martin stood up, "I understand."

They arrived at the police station in Matthias's limousine. The police station, the Lodos Police Department, was a very large and modern-looking building. Matthias smiled a little, "I personally donate quite a sum of money each year so that they have the resources to help as many people as possible. All of these budget cuts are ridiculous." Justin sighed, "Come on. Are we going to report her missing or not?"

A very short man looked up from his desk to the incredibly large man and his normal-sized brothers, "Can I help you?" he asked in a gruff voice. Matthias cleared his throat, "Matthias Delarosa. Captain Root, I suppose?" the short man's eyes widened, and he put a professional smile to his face. "Yes, sir, Captain Ian Root. How can I help you fellows?" Justin stepped forward, "Our young sister has gone missing, sir. She is but seven years old, and quite small for her age. She is in danger." the Captain nodded and stood from his desk, reaching a total height of four feet. He gave a pointed look to Martin, who was quite shocked, "What, too short for you?" Martin shook his head, and the captain grunted, "Come with me, gentlemen." he led them into a conference room and ushered one other officer in there with them. She was the exact height of the captain, with a pointed chin and long, sleek black hair pulled into a low ponytail. She stood next to the captain at the front of the room as the others took their seats.

"Gentlemen, please meet Officer Holly Marx. She is our most promising recruit, and she will personally be assisting your case." Officer Marx nodded, "Any new information will go to me, and then to the Captain, please. I will be in charge of the searching, notices, and informing the public." and she looked straight at Martin, "What's your name, kid?" Martin stood up and bowed slightly, "Martin Anthony Delarosa, ma'am." Officer Marx sat on her right hip, "You look more like a James to me." Captain Root looked at Officer Marx, and then at the boys, "Now, give me a very good, very detailed description, James."

THREE YEARS LATER:

"Holly! Holly, come on, we're going to be late for work." James, who had adopted the nickname (rather by force, because no one would call him differently), was exasperated, waiting for Holly yet again. Holly came out of the coffee shop and handed a cup to James, "Yeah, yeah. Hold your panties, would you? We're fine. It's not like Ol' Root ever yells at us." James shrugged, "You never know. Today could be the day." Holly snorted, "You take this really serious, don't you? Being five minutes late." James sighed, "I have to keep this job, Holly. You know why." Holly sighed, "Yeah, yeah, I know, I know. Blah, blah, blah, find your sister, blah, blah, blah, take back Alacrast, though I don't know why you'd even want to..." James looked to the ground in thought, and Holly put a hand to his arm, "Hey," she said in a softer voice, "It's gonna be okay. We'll find her." James smiled a little, "I know. Come on, I got a page this morning that said there was a murder. Root's gonna want us there."

James sighed and sat down at his desk, head in hands. It wasn't an unusual day, just your typical rob-and-run murder, but it never ceased to take its toll on him. There was a short knock at the door. James looked up to see Holly leaning against the door, "You okay?" James sighed and nodded, "Yeah. Never gets easier, does it?" Holly shook her head, "No, not much. You sure you wouldn't just prefer a desk job?" she snickered as James rolled his eyes.

"Come on," she said, "we've got another call about some street kid." Calls about kids roaming around on the streets, stealing things and loitering and such were common in this city, but they'd been getting more and more frequent.

Holly led James outside, and he tossed her the keys, "Your turn to drive!" Holly rolled her eyes but got in the driver's seat. They passed various corporate buildings that were next to the large complex that made up the law enforcement district. James ran his fingers through his hair, "All these kids…I don't get it. Where are they coming from? Are there really that many runaways?" Holly shrugged, "I don't know, but Root said to be especially wary of this one. Says she's violent, not shy like the others, so watch your back." James snorted, "Please, she's a kid."

Holly shook her head, "She's not that much younger than you. Considerably smaller, but if Root says to be careful, you'd better bet there's a reason. You should know this by now." James had to admit that Holly was right. Root knew better than any of them. "Okay," he agreed, "I'll be careful."

As they arrived on scene, James saw exactly why Root had told them to be careful. This kid was fierce. She was covered completely in black clothes, her thick, flaming red hair tied back into a low ponytail. She was unarmed; her hands and feet were flying through the air, kicking and striking the policemen that were trying to hold her to the ground. She wasn't very strong, but she was fast, and she was smart. Holly gave James a slightly amused look, which he returned, and they exited the car.

"Hey! Hey!" Holly and James ran up to the policemen who were on the side, waiting. "What's going on?" Holly's voice was harsh. The policemen saluted her, "Officer Marx. We caught her trying to steal from a small grocer's store. She tried to run, but we caught her, and she's been fighting them ever since. We've never seen a girl like her. What do you suggest we do?" Holly sighed and looked to James, who rubbed the back of his neck, "Why don't we take her back to the station, see if we can't get her to calm down. Maybe she can give us some information on all these street kids, where they're coming from. It seems like she'll have something to say." Holly looked to the policeman, "You heard him. Get her into the car and down to the station. And make sure she doesn't break anything."

"Let me out of here!" the kid had been banging on the concrete walls of the interrogation room for hours. Her hands were bloody, but when they'd sent in a medic, she'd refused to be touched. James rubbed his temples, "Holly, she's been doing this for three hours. Why don't we just give her something to calm down?" Holly shrugged, "Because first of all, that's illegal. And besides, she's only mad. She's not crazy. I think." James shrugged, "I don't know. This is a little beyond the norm, if you ask me." Holly shook her head and turned towards the door, "I have an idea. Give me a sec." and she went into the room.

James watched from the outside as Holly stood near the door calmly. After a few minutes, the kid noticed that she wasn't alone. She looked at Holly menacingly and commanded, "Let me go." Holly shrugged, "We'll let you go. Once we get you cleaned up and once you talk to us." The girl narrowed her eyes, "What do you want? I can't tell you anything you don't already know." Holly raised an eyebrow, "What do you mean?"

The kid put a hand onto the metal table and started to move her finger around in little circles, "Please. You think I don't know what you're going to ask me? You're going to ask me about the children. And I can't tell you anything you don't already know. I'm useless to you." Holly had not expected this response. She was confused, and was taken aback by the girl's statement, "You know about the children?" the girl snorted, "Of course I know about the children. I'm smarter than you think. And you don't want to mess with me." Holly's breath was uneven and shaky, "Who are you?"

She grinned maliciously, "My name is Kiara Santiago." and without missing a beat, she kicked up and clipped Holly's temple, knocking her unconscious.

Outside the room, James could not believe what he was seeing. A little girl knocking one of the most decorated officers in the system unconscious? The girl was walking out of the room, towards him. Would she attack him as well? What could he do? Was he supposed to hurt this little child, or was he supposed to let her go? He was frozen.

Kiara gave him a vicious smile, "Hello." James tried to speak, but he couldn't. Kiara chuckled, "Tongue-tied, are we? Poor thing. Now listen carefully—you're going to let me go. I am going to walk out of this building untouched and unharmed. Anyone who so much as tries to lay a finger on me will be killed before they realize their mistake. You will leave me alone. And you will leave the children alone, understood?"

James was infuriated, but something about this child scared him. She was plenty smaller than he was—petite, innocent-looking, with big, green eyes and a freckled button nose, so how could she be dangerous? He didn't want to take his chances, though. He'd seen what she did to Holly, and he had no doubt she was true to her word. He didn't say a thing as she walked out of the room and out of the building.

Holly slumped down in her seat and held an ice pack even tighter to her forehead, "I hate that kid." Root snarled, "Don't we all? Now look. She knows about the children. I don't know how she knows—but she does. This could be dangerous. She could be the one taking them." James shrugged, "I don't think she's responsible. I mean, look, she threatened us and told us that she would get them out one way or another. I think she's on our side with this one."

Holly jumped up and winced at the pain, "No street kid is on our side! Ever! They defy the law, they have no concern for safety, they—" A new intern, Felix, stopped her before she said any more, "Come on, Holly, sit down. You're going to give yourself an aneurysm." Holly glared at him, but obliged. Captain Root paced the floor of the conference room, "She's not entirely wrong. They're children, and they've run away for a purpose. It's the hardest thing in the world to gain their trust once they've been hurt to that extent."

James shrugged, "Well, then we gain their trust." Holly looked at him, "I'm sorry? Gain their trust? Our job is to get them to good homes and off the street, not to form relationships." Root nodded, "Holly's right. That's a social workers' job." James nodded and put his hands up, "I know, I know. But if they really do know what's going on with the children, why there's so many of them, maybe they know more than they're letting on. If we gain their trust, we could figure it out. Don't you always say to investigate every possible option? Well, this isn't only possible, but in my eyes, it's plausible. And what if they have Anna? I'm not going to pass up the opportunity to find her."

Holly and Root looked at each other and eventually sighed, "Fine," Root gave in, "if you're so curious, you go. You do this. We'll make it a mission—your first undercover mission. You'll work as a hired hand under your brother. She won't recognize you because it was too dark to see your face in that room. Gain her trust, do whatever you need to do. We'll bug you and get you everything you need." James nodded and smiled triumphantly, "You got it. You're not going to regret this." and as Root stood to leave, he shook his head, muttering, "I hope you're right, kid."

CHAPTER 4:

"Alright, Anya, come on. This is the last one I see."
Anya rushed over to Kiara and helped her drag the wet and
slimy body out of the river. This one was a man with a fat
torso and thinning hair. Kiara grimaced, "You can't just
use other bodies to do your research on? You have to use
the wet, slimy ones from the river?" Anya sighed, "We find
more bodies here, and besides, nobody notices that
someone's taken the dead body anyway. They'd notice if
we took one from a morgue or a more public area."

Anya had been sneaking into the city hall library,
posing as a doctor's daughter sent to get medical books on
how to do procedures and other such things. She had quite
a knack for it, and it was something that distracted her from
her everyday life on the streets. She'd always wanted to be a
doctor, and, well, this was her best chance.

"Roza—I mean, Kiara—how do you think he was
killed?" Kiara looked at the body and crouched down, "See
this thin purple and red gash around his neck? That was a
garrote, a piece of wire attached to two sticks used to cut
someone's throat open and to strangle them. Usually used
by gangs and people who don't want to be caught, so I'd
say he owed someone money. After he was unconscious or
dead, they threw his body into the river so it would be
completely untraceable. They probably threw the murder
weapon in there, too." Anya shook her head, "How do you
know all of that? How can you be so sure?" Kiara gave her

a look, "I just gave you all of my logic! The garrote marks, what it's generally used for, a hypothesis, all of it!"

Anya scoffed, "You should be a police officer. Oh, Officer Santiago! Help me, help me!" Kiara shoved Anya slightly, "Cut it out. I would never be a police officer! Ever! They lie, cheat, steal, beat people…"

"Not to mention they're just plain annoying." a voice said behind them. Both Kiara and Anya whipped around, arms up, ready to fight. What they saw was a young boy Kiara's age, clad in a black cotton jumper suit with his hood down. Kiara narrowed her eyes and put Anya behind her, "Who are you and what do you want?" The boy smiled and stuck out his hand, "I'm Tommy. I want to help you." Kiara looked to Anya, then back to Tommy, "Help? Help with what?" Tommy's smile softened, "You're street kids, right? No home, no food, no clothes besides those? I bet you haven't had a decent meal in weeks." Kiara narrowed her eyes, "That's none of your concern. We're fine on our own. Now leave us alone." Tommy stepped closer and put out a hand, "I can help you!"

Anya lifted her chin in pride, "How?" Tommy put his hands on his hips, "You can come to the Messengers. We're an underground organization of children who are dedicated to the Robin Hood way of life." Anya and Kiara exchanged glances, and Tommy said, "You know, rob from the rich to feed the poor? In exchange for doing missions, we are given food, clothing, and a room and blankets to call our own. Not to mention a home." Kiara sighed, "Look, it sounds a little too good to be true. Thanks, but no thanks. Come on, Anya, let's go." she grabbed Anya's arm and began to walk away from Tommy and towards the drowned bodies.

Tommy stretched out his arm, "Wait! Wait. Please. Just come with me and check it out. If you don't like it, we'll leave you alone." Kiara looked to Anya, who shrugged. Kiara wasn't convinced; things that sounded too good to be true often were. She stole a glance at Anya and took a moment to notice the changes in her. She was more bone than skin, and her once porcelain skin was now sallow. She needed food. Kiara sighed, "Alright, fine. We'll take a look. But just a look." Tommy smiled, "Okay, follow me!"

Mother Messenger, the leader of the Messengers, was a very plump lady. She was draped in robes of painfully clashing bright colors. Her face was pasty ivory, caked in too much makeup. Her hair was almost nonexistent under her elaborate hats covered with feathers. The nails on her fingers were sharp as needles, colored blood red and adorned with jewels that matched the rings on her plump fingers.

She smiled a sickly smile, "Hello, children. And who might you be?" Kiara stepped forward and spoke bravely, "My name is Kiara Santiago. This is my younger sister, Anya. We were brought by Tommy." Mother Messenger opened her arms, "Of course you were. He is my top recruiter. Has he spoken of what we do here?" Kiara nodded slightly, "He said that in exchange for necessities and comfort, we are to perform tasks or missions. What must we do?" Mother Messenger's arms dropped back down to her seat on a pile of jewels and gold trinkets, "Our funds come from various sources. If you can steal, you'll fit in just fine." Kiara looked down at her side. Was this really right? Could she do this? She looked to Anya, who was standing there with an indifferent look on her face. She had to take care of her. She needed more than a cold, makeshift home under a bridge.

"Very well," she spoke with confidence, "I accept." Mother Messenger gave a chuckle, "Perfect! Then I have your first task for you."

Kiara grunted as she lifted herself up onto the last and tallest window ledge. Making sure no one was in the room, she kicked the glass window and slithered through the sharp hole. Pulling her hood up, she ran to the shadows of the torches. Thankful that there was nobody on the top floors due to the party, she made her way silently and stealthily to the ballroom.

Her name is Lady Maria Delarosa. She is the queen of Alacrast's niece. She has long, brown hair, and tanned skin. She is not from this country. You will know who she is.

Kiara remembered Mother Messenger's words as she was given her first task; to assassinate Lady Delarosa. For what reason, she did not know, but she didn't dare ask questions when she and Anya so desperately needed a spot in this organization.

Kiara looked down from a tall balcony and scanned the crowd. Most of the people were fair-skinned and freckled, so it would not be hard to spot a darker-skinned lady.

There she was! Lady Delarosa was smiling brightly, standing next to her husband, Lord Matthias. In the king and queen of Alacrast's absence, they had taken over leadership until the next heir was of age to take the throne.

Kiara drew a poison-tipped arrow out of the quiver on her back, and gaining her balance on the ledge, she took careful aim for the heart. It didn't really matter where she hit her; but the heart would make death quicker, lessening the pain that Lady Delarosa would go through.

She let the arrow fly.

—

"Merry Harvest, my children!" cried Mother Messenger at the Harvest Feast. The children all raised their glasses and yelled in joy, "Merry Harvest!" Anya giggled and looked at the other children her age, who were beckoning her over to their table where they were playing marbles.

Kiara sighed and took a long gulp of her cider. For some reason, she wasn't excited like the others. She didn't feel like celebrating. What was there to celebrate? Two whole years of pillaging, stealing, maiming, and killing? She had not been informed that she would be tasked with killing people when she joined this system, but she had done it anyway. She was disgusted with herself; a killer, a monster. She really was fulfilling her Dark side.

Beyond that, she was sure that Mother Messenger was corrupt. Her sadistic punishments accompanied by her lack of interest with the children, even the sick ones, was beginning to bug Kiara. How could she not help those children, especially when this was all her idea in the first place?

Slowly, she stood up, and walked out of the compound. With the feeling of the cold autumn chill on her face, she began to run. She had to run; it had been so long since she had just run to feel free, to feel in control again. Laughter bubbled up out of her as she jumped over logs and climbed the trees, jumping from limb to limb.

She stopped and jumped down from the trees, landing in a pile of leaves that were crisp and red. She rolled around and let their warmth and autumn scent surround her. She laughed hard and caught her breath, then sat up.

A pair of eyes were on her. They were bright, blue, and wide with fear. They were attached to a handsome body, a dirty blonde head of hair with a clear complexion. He wore a leather jacket and jeans.

Kiara stood quickly and backed up, "Don't scream!" she cried. The boy shook himself out of his stupor and looked confused, "Why would I scream?" Kiara froze. She could not believe what he had just said. She was still in her Messenger uniform. People usually screamed when they saw her, for they knew the horrors of the Messenger organization.

"Who are you?" she asked harshly, "What are you doing here?" the boy looked down in thought, and then stuck out his hand, "I'm James." Kiara looked to his hand and then back to him, "So what are you doing here?" James put his hand down awkwardly, "Uh, I'm…just taking a walk. I think the more appropriate question is what you're doing. Are you even human? I saw you up there in the trees going all Tarzan. What was that all about?" Kiara narrowed her eyes, "Funny. Actually, it's none of your business what I'm doing. Good day."

She pulled her hood up on her cape and started to walk away. James slapped his forehead and groaned to himself before running after her. "Wait!" he cried, "Wait. Wait, I'm sorry. I didn't mean to offend you. Let's start over, shall we? I'm James, just taking a walk around here, nothing weird flying through the trees at all. And your name is…?" he stuck out his hands with a hopeful and nervous smile. Kiara sighed and shook his hand, which fit perfectly into hers, "Kiara."

James smiled, "Kiara. That's kind of pretty." Kiara blushed slightly, then cleared her throat, "I should really be going." and she turned around and began to go. "Wait!" James cried. Kiara turned around in surprise, and then sighed, "Yes?" James smiled, "Stay." Kiara tilted her head, unsure of whether or not this was a trick. James came a little closer, "Don't go. Not just yet." Kiara bravely looked him in the eyes, and despite the color she was sure was rushing to her cheeks, she questioned, "Why?" James looked to the ground, and then back into her eyes with a smile, "Because you're fascinating."

No one had ever called her fascinating before. Kiara was stunned, but she was almost happy. It had been a long time since she had felt that way, and she wanted to continue to feel it. She smiled a little, "Very well. I'll stay." and James' smile widened. He motioned to the trees, "Want to teach me how to do that?" Kiara almost laughed, "What, that? You're much too muscular. You'd have to be quick and agile, and I'm quite sure you're neither." James raised his eyebrows, "Well now. Judgmental a little, aren't we? I'll bet you I'm faster than you." Kiara's face became happily determined with a challenge, "You're on."

—

"Where have you been?" asked Tommy with an angry face. Kiara rolled her eyes as made her way to her Cube. "What's it to you?" Tommy caught up with her and cut off her path, "You've been gone all night. That's not like you." Kiara sighed and pushed him aside, "I went for a walk. Is it a crime to have a life outside of here? Come on, Tommy." Tommy grabbed her arm and spun her around, "Seriously, Kiara. What's wrong with you?" Kiara shrugged, "Can't you tell by now? Everything. Oh, you mean just lately? Well, killing people takes a toll on some people's humanity and dignity. Just some of us, though, obviously."

Tommy, frustrated, huffed out a sigh of annoyance and followed her into her Cube, which consisted of a mattress, oil lamp, an extra cape, and a satchel. Kiara sat down on the mattress and covered her eyes with her hood.

"Look," he said, "it's okay. They deserved it!" Kiara shook her head, but didn't look up, "They didn't deserve it, Tommy. Since when do people deserve to be killed for stupid mistakes? If that were the case, humans wouldn't exist. We would have been extinct eons ago." Tommy sighed and sat down next to her, "Kiara, people die. This is what happens to people who can't keep their promises to us."

"I don't care!" she burst out. Tommy flinched as Kiara ripped back her hood, "I don't care. What does it matter what they did? I killed a person, I killed people! People with families, with children, with friends and a job and a life! I took away a life! That is not my duty. That is not something that I am supposed to do! I—I'm just a kid, Tommy." Tommy nodded and touched her arm, "I know, Kiara. We all are. But you can't be a kid anymore. You have to take care of Anya. And, Kiara, listen." he looked around and opened the curtain, making sure no one was listening.

"You need to overthrow Mother Messenger." Kiara snapped up, "What?" Tommy sighed, "You need to get her out. Kiara, she's getting less and less supplies for the kids, there's almost no food left in the bank. Winter is coming and we have no blankets or firewood. She doesn't care about the kids anymore. All she cares about is how much money and jewelry is coming in." Kiara was baffled, "But why me?" Tommy took her hands, "All the kids look to you. You're the oldest here beyond me. You can fight better than anyone I've ever seen, and you're not afraid to stand up to her. You have to take over the Messengers."

Kiara stood up, "I can't! I can't lead people, I don't know the first thing about leading someone, not to mention an entire organization! There's no way!" Tommy stood with her, "Kiara, get a grip. You can do this. You were born to, I've seen you; you're a natural leader and you do so well under stressful situations, and you look out for these kids like they're your own. You have to." Kiara was torn into pieces. This was all so sudden, and before Tommy could protest, she ran from the room and accidentally stumbled into Anya. Anya looked up from the ground to Kiara, angry at first, and then worried. "Kiara?" she asked as she stood, "Are you alright?" Kiara sniffled and kept the tears from flowing out of her eyes, "Yes. I um…I just need to go."

Anya smiled softly, "I'm coming with you." and she took Kiara's hand as they walked through the empty sewer complex to the city above. Anya looked at Kiara, "What did Tommy say?" Kiara sat down against a tree and rolled her eyes, "He wanted me to overthrow Mother Messenger." Anya's jaw dropped, "Overthrow her? As in kill her?" Kiara shrugged, "I don't know. Probably. It's not like there's any other way. He had good reasons; great reasons, but I'm not the person he should be going to." Anya was confused, "What do you mean? Kiara, you'd be a great leader!" Kiara snorted, "Yeah, right. Look at me. I can barely take care of you, Anya, let alone a bunch of other kids. And beyond that, I abandoned my kingdom." Anya took her hands, "Kiara, they wanted to kill you. You know that they were after you that night. You had to leave!"

Kiara stood, "And now I can never go back. Look at me, with my record now…" Anya shrugged, "It's not your fault. It's your job. They know what they'll get if they don't comply to our terms." Kiara glared at her, "Yes, it is my fault! I could have chosen not to! Once I saw how corrupt this stupid organization was, I could have left with you. I never had to take an innocent life. Their blood is on my hands. I can't ever wash that off! I am not fit to govern these people if I can't determine between right and wrong!" Anya sighed, "You're fifteen years old. You're just a kid." Kiara turned her back to Anya, putting a hand against a tree to steady herself, and thought back to what Tommy had said. She sighed, "I can't be a kid anymore." and off she ran through the woods.

Tommy grabbed Anya by the arm in panic, "Where's Kiara?" Anya shrugged, "I don't know. She ran off." Tommy groaned, "Ran off? Why?" Anya pulled her arm away in anger, "Because you told her she couldn't be a kid anymore! What's wrong with you? Why do you have to put all that responsibility on her? If it's so important to you, do it yourself! Don't get someone else to do the dirty work for you!" and off she stormed.

Kiara screamed in anger and threw another rock into the lake. She grunted and sat down, trying not to pull her fiery hair from its roots.

"You okay?" Kiara jumped up, ready to fight. She rolled her eyes and put down her fists as she noticed that it was James. She went back to her position on the ground, "What do you want?" James snorted, "Nice to see you too. Thanks for the concern, James. Oh, no problem, Kiara!" She rolled her eyes again, "Can I help you, or are you just here to mock me?" James sat down next to her, "I'm not trying to mock you. But seriously, are you okay? Do you want to talk about it?" Kiara shook her head, "Nothing's wrong. I'm fine." James nodded, "Well, then, if nothing's wrong, you won't object to coming with me." Kiara gave him a dubious look, "Come with you? Where?" she suddenly leaped up, afraid, "No! You stay away from me! Don't you dare touch me!"

James was shocked and stood up slowly, "No, no, Kiara, it's okay. It's okay. I'm not going to do anything to you. I wanted to know if you wanted to go for a walk. I was thinking you could show me around the forest. You seem to know it pretty well." Kiara's breathing slowed and her eyes became less wild. She nodded, "Oh. Yeah. Sure." James smiled, "Let's go, then."

The woods were chilly, and as James and Kiara walked, they were silent. James was unsure of what to say. What should he ask her? Should he ask her anything at all? Or should he just let it be silent? Kiara was content with the silence, but unused to having anyone but Anya or Tommy walk beside her.

Without a word, James turned to her, "Kiara, I have a surprise for you." Kiara looked him up and down, confused, "A surprise? What?" James laughed, "Close your eyes and hold out your hands." Kiara was wary, but she did as she was told, and cried out as metal clamped around her wrists.

"Aah!" she cried, opening her eyes. There were guards all around her, and James' face had gone from playful to menacing, "You're under arrest for the murder of Lady Maria Delarosa." Kiara growled and tried to run, but these men were too strong, and they shackled her legs.

"What the hell, James?" she cried. James looked back and Kiara could have sworn she saw sorrow, "She's my cousin. My cousin sent me to find you. I'm sorry."

Kiara couldn't believe how stupid she'd been as she was carried to a boat and taken across the canal that separated Alacrast and Lodos. She had never thought in a million years that she would be back on this dark land.

Victor. Tallah. Perhaps they were still here! If they were…she could howl. They would come find her. She would be free.

Kiara waited patiently until they reached land, and when she was motioned to get off the boat, she pleaded, "Please, can you take these off? They hurt, and my ankles will bleed soon." The guard gave her a nasty look, "Hush! Stop your complaints!" but James came to her side, "Of

course, Kiara. But you have to stay with us." Kiara nodded
and gave James her most sincere and innocent look, "I
promise." James motioned for a guard to unshackle her. As
soon as she was free of chains and on the ground, she
bolted.

It had been so long since she had changed into a wolf,
but she let herself run faster than the wind and take her
graceful form. Without looking back, she darted into the
forest, knowing that she had lost them.

"Who are you?" an aggressive voice cried as she was
tackled to the ground. Kiara wrestled back, "Get off me!"
and was pinned to the ground. She looked into the golden
eyes of a fierce wolf, and relaxed, "Victor?" the wolf let her
up and backed away, "How do you know my name?" Kiara
smiled, "Victor, it's me, Kia—Roza. It's Roza."

Victor's eyes widened in shock, "Roza? We…we were
told we'd never see you again, that you'd gone to be the
queen in Lodos." Kiara shook her head, "No, they tried to
assassinate me. I ran away. It's been complicated." Victor
shook his head, "Well, what are you doing here?" Kiara
looked around, "I was captured and taken here because I
killed Lady Delarosa." Victor's jaw dropped, "You're the
one who killed Lady Delarosa?" Kiara nodded, "Yes."

"Why?" he asked, circling her in amazement. Kiara
shrugged, "I was told to. But never mind that. Where's
Tallah?" Victor stopped and motioned to the bushes behind
him, "He's back with the pack. I was just wandering
around. Wait, Roza, look out!" Victor pushed her out of

the way in panic. Kiara cried out in shock and landed on her side. She looked up to see Victor growling and barking at the guards she had most recently escaped from. "Victor!" she yelled, "Run! Go! Now!" Two guards grabbed her and lifted her up. Victor turned to run towards her, but Kiara growled, "Go! Victor, go! Now! That's an order!" Victor looked around and knew he was outnumbered. With a last glance back, he darted off into the woods.

Kiara lost all of her energy and let herself turn back into a human in raggedy clothing. She stood still as James came up to her, "What the hell was that?" he demanded. Kiara spat at his feet, "I will always fight for my freedom." James looked at her in disgust, "Take her to the dungeon. Matthias will decide what to do with her."

Kiara sat in the cold, wet dungeon. It was hard stone, and it was even harder to see where anything was. There was a bit of straw, and rats milling around. The guards thrust grits and water towards her. Kiara spat in it and spilled it over. "The King has been generous!" one of them yelled. Kiara grimaced with anger, "I beg to differ."

"Do you now?" a calm voice came in. It was James. "If someone had killed my wife, I might have tracked them down myself and killed them on the spot. This is a luxury for someone like you." Kiara diverted her eyes, "Someone like me?" James smirked, "A murderess. A coward. Someone without feeling."

"It's people like you who force us to be like this!" she cried and slammed herself against the bars of her cell.

James narrowed his eyes, "Us? There are more of you?" Kiara's breathing stopped for a second, long enough for James to notice.

"Someone get Root! Bring him here immediately; tell him it's an emergency." There was a collective, "Yes, sir!" and the guards clanked away. James paced the floor, "So there's more of you. You're the one who's been stealing them. We were right!" Kiara shook her head, "Wait…we? Right? You're with the police!" Kiara realized how stupid she'd been to trust this man she knew nothing about and slammed her fist into the cold, hard stone.

"Hey, cut it out! We need you alive at least." Kiara snarled and looked to the corner where she'd been playing with rope earlier. There were hooks on the ceiling to hang food to torture crippled guests of the dungeon. Knowing James' back was turned, she picked up the rope and leapt onto the wooden bed, just high enough for her to reach one of the hooks. She tied the rope around it and formed the other end into a loop. She was light enough that her neck would snap if she jumped hard enough. She put the noose around her neck and sat on the bed. Silently, she waited.

"Alright, what's the emergency? Why is it so dark? Can someone please get some light down here?" a gruff voice was yelling out commands and questions with an air of authority. Kiara knew that this must be 'Root,' whoever that was.

James quickly had the guards light torches and was shocked to see her with a noose around her neck. Root ran over, "Hey! What's she doing? Who's...?" Root realized who she was. Kiara recognized him from the day she was interrogated. He was the Captain, the man-in-charge. Root looked at James, "Why is there a noose around her neck?" James' eyes were wide in surprise, and he struggled to speak, "What?" he turned his attention to Kiara, "Don't move! Just take the noose off! Don't do this!" Kiara shrugged, "I won't. If you let me go."

Root sighed, "We will. Maybe. After some questions. Now what's this all about?" James pointed at her, "There are more like her." Root nodded, "Yeah. Street kids. We know. Your point?" James shook his head, "No. They're trained like she is." Root turned around, "I thought this was all about gaining her trust." James raised his eyebrows for a second, "It was. Until she killed my cousin. That plan kind of went out the window after that." Root nodded, "Good point. She killed your cousin?" James nodded, "Poisoned arrow straight to the heart. She was seen only after the deed was done. No one heard or saw her come in. She's a trained assassin." Root looked at James like he was stupid, "She's twelve!"

"Thirteen." commented Kiara.

"She's thirteen!" he cried, "She can't possibly be a trained assassin!" James shrugged, "Well, she is. She left her fingerprints on the arrow. We know because we fingerprinted her as routine when we brought her in for questioning." Root nodded, "Well, Miss...?" Kiara stood, "Santiago." Root backed up and put his hands up, "Alright, then, Miss Santiago, calm down there. Don't move." Kiara smiled ruefully, "Are you daring me?" James sighed, "Look, who are the others? What did you mean?" Kiara sighed, "I won't tell you."

"Why not?" questioned Root, "Whatever it is, we'll keep you safe. Don't worry." Kiara snorted, "They're my family! We're all a family! I will never tell you. Now let me go!" James shook his head, "We can't do that, Kiara."

Root walked towards her calmly, "Were you stolen? It's okay. It's not your fault. We can get you back to your mom and dad. It will all be okay." At the mention of her parents, Kiara felt a lump in her throat as hot tears ran down her face. "My parents are dead. I ran away. I wasn't stolen. You're the ones who are stealing all the kids! You just don't want to admit it!"

Before James or Root could say another word, they both slumped to the ground. There stood Victor and Tallah with bricks from the loosened cells in their hands. Kiara took the noose off of her neck and ran towards them as they unlocked her cell.

"Tallah!" she cried as he embraced her. Tallah picked her up and swung her around, "Oh, Rosebud, I missed you so much! Never leave us again!" Kiara let him go, "We haven't got time. I have to get back to Lodos. They're stealing children." Victor gave her a look, "Stealing children?" Kiara nodded, "They've been disappearing from everywhere. No one knows where they've gone, and they're disappearing at a really fast pace. I'm part of an organization that protects runaways, but it's becoming more and more corrupt. You have to help me." Tallah nodded, "Anything for our best friend. What do we do?"

—

"Alright, Tallah, you know what to do. Distract the kids. Make sure they don't see." Tallah nodded, "You got it." and with Tommy's help, he ran off. Victor and Anya looked to me, "This is going to be quick and painless. You two cover me from her guards. It'll be a surprise attack, so I need them unconscious. Got it?" Victor and Anya nodded and ran off as well. Kiara sat against the wall of her Cube and sighed, preparing herself. She would go in, unarmed, and get as close as possible. When it was least expected, she would strike.

Kiara stood and walked calmly to the Throne Room, where Mother Messenger was too busy counting her jewels to notice that her guards were missing. When Kiara cleared her throat, Mother Messenger looked up and smiled, "Kiara! How can I help you, my dear?" Kiara smiled sweetly, "I just…I just wanted to thank you. In private." Mother Messenger motioned for Kiara to come closer, "Whatever do you mean, my child?" Kiara stood next to her, "I mean, you gave my sister and I a home. She's happy now, and it's all thanks to you." Mother Messenger smiled, "Of course, my sweet. That is what we're meant to do, to fix people's broken lives." Kiara's smile faded, "Of course." and without another word, Kiara spun around and kicked the woman's temple. Mother Messenger slumped to the ground. Kiara could still feel a pulse as she pressed her fingers to the woman's jugular.

"Victor! Anya!" she cried. The two came running out, "She's still alive. Give her the poison. You know where to take her." Victor nodded and called to Tallah, "Come on, Tal!" Tallah came running out of the other room and without a question, he helped Victor take away the large woman. Kiara looked to Anya, "Go explain to the children. We're starting anew here." Anya smiled, "Yes, O Queen of the Streets."

CHAPTER 5:

Kiara snuck in through the window and looked around. The coast was clear, and as far as she knew, no one was awake. She'd scanned this place for days. Kody, a friend of Anya's, was in the west wing, right across from the fourth window. All she had to do now was find him.

Kiara crept around and climbed up the creaking stairs, sometimes even taking it as far as to walk on the rickety railing so as not to be heard. She went westward, and was almost caught by two night guards, but thankfully, a thrown rock saved her.

She hurried over to Kody's still body, laid a hand over his mouth, and shook him. His eyes opened wide in fear, but she shushed him, "Shh, shh. It's me. Come on, let's go." Kody sat up and nodded to the corner, where four other children came out of the shadows, "I'll explain later," he said, "they're street kids, too." Kiara nodded, "Okay. Let's go." She went over to the window and whistled. Immediately, two figures in black tossed a hook that was attached to a rope up to the window. Kiara secured it and held up a hand with all five fingers extended. They nodded back and prepared to catch the children. Kiara helped them onto the rope and told them, "Now slide down," and one by one, they safely reached the ground. Kody went last, and as soon as he reached the ground, someone touched Kiara's shoulder. She turned around suddenly, and was surprised to find a small child reaching up towards me. Kiara crouched down, "And who are you?" she asked her. She was holding a stuffed bunny and sucking her thumb. She couldn't have been more than five.

"Linny." she said, and Kiara looked at her, "Linny, do you have parents?" she shook her head no. Kiara smiled, "Then come with me." Linny nodded happily, and whispered to her, "Are you Kiara?" Kiara laughed softly and nodded, "Yes." Linny smiled even more and hugged her rescuer, and Kiara was about to help Linny down the rope when she heard boot steps.

"Hey! You! What are you doing? Stop!" the guard blew his whistle, and within seconds, they were surrounded. Kiara pushed Linny back and took out her daggers. "Stand back!" she yelled, and they looked at her daggers warily. Kiara grabbed Linny and told her, "Down the rope!" and she nodded and did as she was told.

One of the guards grabbed Kiara's arm, but she was on top of him in a second, and clipped his temple with the side of her hand. It turned into a brawl within moments. She flipped around, arms and legs flying, her daggers slashing skin and drawing blood, sometimes even her own. In a minute, they were all down. Kiara breathed in and out heavily, and slid down the rope.

"Alright, let's go!" she cried, and without hesitation, they were gone.

"Mistress Kiara!" one of the Messengers came to her, "Our month's shipment of food has just come in!" Kiara nodded and kept walking, "Good." another called to her,

"Mistress Kiara, where are the extra blankets for the sick room?" she looked to a shipment paper and signed her name, "Third closet to the left in the supplies room." the girl nodded and ran off. Another boy came to her and said, "Mistress Kiara, your mail has arrived." and handed her a bundle of letters. She looked up from the floor and cried, "Can nobody just call me Kiara like I've been asking every day for two years?" the Messengers looked down in guilt, "Yes, Kiara." they said in unison. She nodded, "Thank you."

"Busy today?" asked Tommy as he handed her an apple. Kiara gratefully took a bite, "Yeah. Lots of stuff coming in, that's all. How's the other side going?" Kiara had recently put Victor and Tallah in charge of a new Messenger organization in Alacrast. Tommy nodded, "As far as I know, it's going well. Getting started still, but it's getting there." Kiara nodded, "Good. I need you to handle the rest of today's affairs. I'm taking a personal night." Tommy smiled and clapped her on the back, "You got it! Don't get too crazy, okay?" Kiara rolled her eyes and chuckled, "Whatever you say, Tommy."

Kiara passed Anya and hugged her quickly, then went to her Cube, grabbed her cloak, and headed out of the underground complex.

—

"That's the fifth report this month." Holly, Gabriel, the new cop, James, his assistant, Rose, Felix, and Captain Root were all sitting at the bar around a table with papers in front of them. Felix sighed, "Maybe she's trying to make a statement." Gabriel snorted, "A statement? Like what? Save the kids! I think she's just trying to show off and take them for herself." Captain Root shook his head, "I don't think so. I think she really believes she's saving these kids."

"From who?" asked Rose, "Last I heard, the leader of the Messengers was dead. Kiara killed her." Holly nodded, "Then that would automatically make her head of the Messengers. What is she doing, and where is she? Even our dogs, our machines, our Sensors can't find her. She's all around, but she's nowhere! So how is she pulling all of this off?" Holly looked at James, "James? You haven't said a word all day. What are you thinking about?" James looked at Holly, "Nothing. It's nothing." Holly shrugged, "Whatever you say." and took a drink of her beer. Rose looked at James and sighed, and then looked around the bar.

"Um, guys," she patted Felix and James urgently. They both looked up at her, "What?" they asked, annoyed. She grunted and nodded towards a cloaked figure at the bar, talking to one of the bartenders. He nodded, and gave the figure a glass with red liquid in the bottom, clear liquid on top, and a cherry. The coworkers exchanged glances. They didn't need to say anything to know that it was Kiara. The cloaked figure downed the drink in one gulp, pushed back the glass, left a few coins, and turned around, her cape swirling and exposing a flash of red hair.

She left, and everyone panicked. They all stood up and went outside as quickly as possible, slamming some money down on the table.

"There she is!" Felix whispered to the rest of them, pointing to the cloaked person crossing the street. James zipped up his coat, "I'm going after her." Captain Root nodded, "Be careful, Delarosa. And if you want a raise, you'll bring her back with you." James nodded, "See you guys." he followed the cloaked figure far out of town to a lake.

Kiara sighed and took off her cloak and Messenger's uniform to reveal her undershorts and tank top. She stepped briskly into the warm water and smiled at the sensation of the sand beneath her feet and the warm breeze against her skin and in her hair. It had been so long since she had felt so at peace. There was nothing that could ruin her mood at this point.

"Kiara." a voice said. Kiara whipped around and saw James standing there. She narrowed her eyes and thought twice about her previous claim. "James." she said, unamused, "It's been a long time." James nodded, "Two years. We've been looking all over for you, but you've been off the radar." Kiara shrugged, "I've been keeping my distance. Figured it would be best after your little stunt in the woods." James shrugged, "Probably. You're wanted for murder, among other things." Kiara nodded, "Yeah, that kind of comes with this sort of life. Have you forgiven me yet?" James sighed, "To be honest, I never liked her anyway. Too consumed in herself for Matthias."

Kiara took a step deeper into the water, "So what do you want?" James looked at her inquisitively, "I...I don't know, really." Kiara raised an eyebrow, "Then what are you doing here?" James sighed, "I wanted to talk to you." Kiara turned around and moved her leg around in the water, "What about?"

James shrugged, "It's weird. When I'm not around you, I'm logical and I know that I should arrest you, but then I look at you and..." Kiara took another step back, "And what?" James shook his head, "I look at you and all I want to do is help you." Kiara narrowed her eyes, "I'm not some sorry little puppy, you know. I can take care of myself." James nodded and smiled, amused, "Yes, I'm quite aware of that. I meant that...I want to help you in your cause. You're doing something that's good, but you're doing it in the wrong way." Kiara shrugged, "Only according to people like you. And don't even think you can just...switch sides." James laughed slightly, "I know, it's just..." he sighed, "Kiara, you've bewitched me."

Kiara's eyes widened, "What? What do you mean?" James took off his shoes and socks and rolled up his pants, stepping into the water, "I think you know what I mean." Kiara took a step back, the water up to her thighs, almost touching her shorts, "Don't even think about trying anything!" James put his hands up, "No! No! I'm sorry. I just...can I ask you something?" Kiara nodded slightly, still on edge. James sighed and rubbed his hands over his face, "Who are you? Really? Beneath the street kid thing. Who were you before? I want to know." Kiara relaxed, "Why?" James stepped out of the water and sat down on the sand, "Because I didn't join this cop business to arrest people or to catch criminals or anything like that." Kiara looked him up and down warily, "Then why did you?" James looked into the water, "I joined it to find my little sister. She's been missing for five years. Everyone says she's dead, but I know she's not. I can feel it." Kiara nodded and sat next to him, but not too close, "I have a little sister, too. Every day she gets a little sadder. I suppose it's because life isn't getting much better for us."

James turned to her, "So who were you before all this started? What happened?" Kiara sighed, "I was born into nobility. Someone killed my parents when I was a baby. After that, I moved in with other nobility. At my adoptive sisters' birthday party, the same people who killed my parents tried to kill me. My adoptive brother told me to take Anya, run, and never return, so I did. We were pulled into an orphanage, but they tried to separate us, so we ran away and stayed on the streets. I couldn't take the risk of us being separated. She's all I've got." James looked at her, his face a mix of sorrow and appreciation, "Kiara, I…I'm so sorry. I, too, was forced out of my home." Kiara raised an eyebrow, "How come?" James sighed, "Wolves attacked and killed my parents. My mother told us to run, so my brother, sister, and I did. My brother took a different path and lives with Matthias now, but when I was trying to escape with Anna, she was taken."

Kiara stood, "Did you say wolves? Where did you used to live?" James stood with her, "Yes, wolves. Alacrast, in the palace. I'm the uh—prince." Kiara looked to the ground, her eyes wide with fear, "How long ago?" James shrugged, "Six years." Kiara picked up her clothing, "I've got to go." James ran after her and grabbed her arm, "Why?" and he turned her around. When he saw her green eyes glint in the moonlight, he recognized them for just a second.

"Wait a minute…" he started, "you aren't…you can't be a…" Kiara nodded, "Wolf." and without looking back, she ran.

—

James pushed open the doors to the Lodos Police Department and slammed them shut. He threw his coat on his chair and angrily paced the floor. Holly, Root, Gabriel, Felix, and Rose all watched in shock and silence.

"Um, James…" Rose spoke first, "Are you alright?" James seethed, "No. No, I'm not alright. She killed them. She's a wolf. She killed them." Holly stepped forward, "Wolf? Who else did she kill?" James wiped silent tears from his eyes, "My parents." Rose gasped, and Gabriel stepped forward in anger, "That evil little—" Rose clapped a hand over Gabriel's mouth, "Watch it." she warned. James grabbed Gabriel's collar, "What were you going to call her?" the entire building paused for a second as each of the group members realized what James was saying. He was protecting her. Rose took her hand away from Gabriel's mouth, "James…are you mad at her, or at Gabriel?"

James sat down on his desk, "I don't know. I should be mad at her, but I can't be." Gabriel shook his head, "James, this just confirms that she's bad news." James shook his head, "No, you guys, she's not bad. She's…she's lost. She told me her story, and she seemed so sad. She really thinks that this is the only way she can live in safety. She was about to be assassinated, that's why she's a runaway. She's hiding for her life. Forget about my parents. There's nothing we can do about them. We need to help her."

Felix rubbed his head, "So we're supposed to help the girl that killed your parents and your cousin?" Holly stepped forward, "Okay, I think you had a little too much to drink. Maybe we should just call it a night." James' glare cut her like a knife, "No. I know what I'm saying. She needs help. We have to help her." Rose stepped in front of Holly, "How?" James sighed, "We need to find out who she is. We need to find out who tried to assassinate her and why. She said she was nobility and that her parents were assassinated as well. Felix, look up every assassination of nobility in the last sixteen years. That'll put it a year before she was born at least."

Without a question, Felix did as he was told. James turned to Holly, "Contact all nobility you can, see if we can

weed out any bad apples, some family feuds or something."
Holly was about to protest, but Root stopped her with a
look, "Do it." he turned to James, "What can I do?" James
sighed, "Help Felix. Narrow down the search. It needs to
be around the year she was born." Root nodded, "Yes, sir."
Gabriel sighed, "I'll help Holly."

Rose gave James a tiny smile, "So you forgive her?"
James stood up, "Something tells me that killing my
parents wasn't an act of cold blood. Besides, I don't even
know if it was her. For all I know, it could have been part
of her...pack." he was still getting used to the idea of Kiara
being a wolf. Rose put up her hands in question, "So how
do you know it was her who was at least there?" James
leaned back and his eyes became dreamy, "Her eyes.
They're like emeralds. I've only seen eyes so bright once.
Besides, I almost killed her. I owe her."

Rose didn't ask any more questions the rest of the
night.

———

"Kiara?" Tommy put the papers he was holding into
someone else's hands and followed her as she dashed off to
her Cube, "Kiara, what's wrong?" Kiara flung herself down
on her bed, exhausted emotionally and physically. Tommy
crouched down next to her, "What's wrong?"

"It's him." Tommy shook his head, "I'm not
following." Kiara ran her fingers through her tangled hair,
"James. I know him. I—I was his friend as a child. Back in

Alacrast. And then I attacked him with the rest of the wolf pack and now he knows. He's going to want to kill me."

Tommy raised an eyebrow, "Why would you care if he wants to kill you?" and with some realization, he stood up, "Oh, no! No, no! Don't even let me think that!" Kiara looked up at him with sad eyes, "Think what?" Tommy almost glared at her, "You don't like him, do you?" Kiara's eyes went wild and she leapt up in defense, "What? Of course not! That's absurd!" Tommy pointed a finger at her, "It better be. You know our rules. They're there for a reason." and without a word, he left.

Kiara sunk to the floor. That couldn't possibly be true. She hated him! She had to hate him, didn't she? He was a cop, and furthermore, he was part of the royalty of Alacrast, the people who had banished the wolves. He was evil! He was...

He was not evil. He had captured her those years ago out of anger. She'd have done the same thing, and she probably wouldn't have been so lenient with letting her go after he had the chance to capture her again. And he just kept coming back! Why did he keep coming back? Why did he have to complicate things? Before he'd shown up, she had one purpose, and now, all of that was changing.

Kiara couldn't believe what she was thinking. Changing? Nothing was changing. She was still the same as she had been. Her goals hadn't changed, her morals hadn't changed, nothing had changed. He was still the policeman who was trying to bring her to "justice" and she was still the rebel vagabond.

Was he really all that bad, though? He hadn't been angry when she told him about being a wolf. He hadn't tried to hurt her. He hadn't tried to capture her. He just wanted to talk. And she ran away. Again.

Anya poked her head in, "Kiara?" Kiara snapped her head up, startled, "Hey, come in." Anya sat down across from her, "Tommy told me." Kiara shook her head, "Told you what?" Anya looked to the ground, "That you like James." Kiara reminded herself to behead Tommy in the morning.

She sighed, "I don't like James. I'm just confused. I have a lot of mixed feelings. But I don't like him. He's a cop. I can't like him." Anya nodded, "Exactly. You're not supposed to, but then, you've always been one for breaking rules." Kiara shook her head, "Anya, what do I do?" Anya took her hands, "We don't belong here, Kiara. We never have. You're supposed to be leading this country, not its underground." Kiara sighed, "I know. But I have to fix this system first. After that…then we'll discuss it." Anya nodded and stood, "Of course." Kiara was confused, "What? What's wrong?" Anya shrugged angrily, "Oh, I don't know. I'm just wondering when the hell we're going to get out of here and live the lives we're supposed to." Kiara stood up, facing her, "This is our life. We have to be here."

Anya shoved her away, "Maybe you do, but I never asked for this! You really think those people are still after us? You really think they'll pull another stunt like the ball?" Kiara resisted the urge to shove her back, "You don't know! I don't know, but I don't want to take that chance!" Anya rolled her eyes, "You know, you talk a big game, but at the end of the day, you're just scared. And I don't even think you're scared of them hurting me, I think that you're scared that it will be your fault! Poor Kiara, everything's on her! Well guess what? It's not! I live my own life! You don't have to take care of me!" Kiara took a step towards her and put a hand on her shoulder, "Yes, I do. You're my sister. It's my job to protect you and take care of you." Anya violently whipped her sister's hand away, "Oh, don't try to pull that rubbish with me! You're so focused on spiting the police and taking kids off the streets to care about me! Why don't you do me a favor and just leave me alone?" Anya gave her one last nasty glance and stormed out of her sister's cube.

Kiara was stunned. It was rare for Anya to be so enraged, and it scared her. Was Anya right? Did she pay too much attention to the others? Well, she had to. There were a hundred kids that looked to her for protection. She had to focus her attention on them. Anya could be trusted to take care of herself for the most part. She needed to clear her thoughts.

Kiara pulled on her cloak and left the Messengers, heading down a back alleyway, looking for a place to think.

She turned right down a less-known alley, but was stopped in her tracks by a group of unseemly men.

"Hey, little girl," one man called, "whatcha doin' out here, all alone?"

"You need someone to keep you company?"

"We're real good company," There were at least six of them. Big, burly, adults with unshaven skin and sweaty scents. They were either a really bad gang, or prison escapees. Either way, it was trouble for her. She may have been a good fighter, but that's with Anya at her side, and with daylight. With the darkness, outnumbered six to one, and without a partner, Kiara was toast.

They came closer to her, huddling around her. One of them touched her backside, and she bit towards him, "Don't touch me!"

"Look at her, she's so cute!"

"A feisty little one, isn't she?"

Kiara tried to fight her way out of their grasps, but she couldn't. They had her locked. She kicked her leg up and hit one of them in the face, hoping to get a chance to escape. She may not have been as strong, but she was definitely faster.

They didn't like that. They punched back, trying to get hold of her. They were trying to touch her, and she was screaming out, but no one came. She was all alone. A wolf with no pack.

"AAH!" one of them raked their ring across her face. It hurt and burned and stung. Kiara could feel red, sticky blood flow down her face, her skin searing with pain. She didn't dare open her eyes for fear that blood would flow into them. She screamed so loud that soon, she could hear sirens getting closer. Police and an ambulance. *No! No, they can't take me! NO!* But she didn't have the strength to get up. The gang must have heard the sirens, too, because the next thing she knew, they were high-tailing out of there.

"Miss? Miss, are you conscious?" someone picked her up and she sniffed and nodded. She would hold in her sobs, no matter how much it hurt.

"Katherine, get her into the ambulance, now! She's losing a lot of blood." Someone else took her, and the last thing Kiara remembered was listening to the faint sound of her own breathing and her heartbeat, calming her down.

—

"I think we've got something!" Felix stood up, followed by Root, and handed a piece of paper to James, "Here. Fifteen years ago, about a month after Kiara would've been born. The king and queen of Lodos had gone to a remote island. No one knew why. They were killed there. Their bodies were found in the basement. Their children were gone."

"Children? If they're Kiara's parents, she's an only child." Felix shrugged, "Everything matches up. The people who were arrested and convicted of attempted assassination of the current royal family has the same pattern as the people who assassinated the former king and queen. Fingerprints and DNA from the crime scenes confirm it." Root sighed, "That means that our street kid is the rightful heir to the throne." Holly chose this time to step in, "That doesn't mean that she's excused from her crimes." James shook his head, "No, but I don't think she knows that she's not being hunted anymore. Let me see these birth records."

James read the birth records of Roza Kiara Collins and Rowan Seamus Collins. They were twins. But why had their family gone into hiding? "Root!" he called. Root came to his side, "Yeah?" James rubbed the back of his neck in thought, "See if you can find out why the last family went AWOL all of a sudden. Contact the royal family and tell them we have their adoptive daughter. And we need Rowan, wherever he is. Also tell all the local police that if they see Kiara to calmly approach her as a royal and to bring her back." Root nodded, "Got it."

As Root made the call, he motioned James over with wide eyes. "Thanks," he said into the phone, and rushing to get his coat, he yelled, "Come on! She's in the hospital, she was attacked. Let's go!"

"Kiara!" James cried out as he entered the hospital. A nurse came up to them, "I assume you're all here for the girl with the red hair?" when they nodded, the nurse pointed down the hall, "Go in gently. She's in a rough state, but she'll be alright. She doesn't look so good, so be careful. I suggest one at a time, and quietly, please."

James nodded, "Thanks," and rushed down the hall. He knocked lightly, and entered the room. The first thing he noticed was the huge, red scar that ran diagonally across her face. "Kiara!" he rushed to her side and sat down on the bed next to her, "What happened?" Kiara leaned back, "Wrong alleyway. Couldn't get away from them." James took her hand, "I'm so glad you're alright." Kiara looked at him, "James…" she questioned, "why?" he gave her a look, "Why what?" Kiara sniffled, "Why do you like me? Look at me. I'm just a street kid. What could you possibly see in me?" James squeezed her hand pressed a letter into it, "You're a fighter. I admire that. There's just something about you…you've bewitched me, Kiara. This is for you." Kiara pushed his hand away, "You can't like me. You can't." James was confused, "What do you mean?"

"Kiara?" the door opened, and Kiara looked towards the door. It was Root. She raised an eyebrow, "Yes?" another head popped in, a girl with brown hair and a soft face. Rose's eyes widened as she realized who this girl was.

"Roza?" Rose whispered. Kiara tried to look at her more closely, and said, "Rose?" without hesitation, she was wrapped in a fierce, painful hug, but she didn't care about the pain. She hugged her back just as fierce. "Oh, Roza," she said, "I missed you so much!" she was crying, and Kiara was trying her best not to. "I missed you, too," she whispered. "I missed you, too."

James and Root were confused. Root broke the two up, "What is going on here?" he cried, and Rose shrugged, "You never told me it was her! I've never seen a picture of Kiara. I didn't know it was Roza!" Kiara laughed slightly,

"You could have guessed! How did you get out of the orphanage?" Rose smiled, "I found a foster family and got a job with them. I graduated high school early and they offered me a job full-time as a secretary." Kiara shook her head, "I told you that you were a genius." Rose shrugged, "Anya's the genius. I'm just determined. Are you okay? What happened to you?" Kiara shook her head, "Just a fight. Don't worry about it. I'm just glad you're okay." Rose nodded and hugged her friend, "Get some rest, okay? We'll be back." Kiara nodded and laid back on the pillows and propped up bed, closing her eyes and letting sleep wash over her.

"So, how exactly do you two know each other?" James gave Rose a strange look as they walked down the long hallways. Rose looked up at him, then quickly down at the floor, "She's...she's my old best friend. We met in an orphanage before I found my foster family. You guys don't have a picture of Kiara, so I never knew that they were the same person." she said timidly. James nodded, "Right. Okay. Why don't you and I go and see the doctor?" Rose nodded, and together, they walked down the hall. Felix stopped them, "Guys," his eyes were wide with shock, "You've gotta investigate this."

Days later, Kiara was released and roaming the streets again, looking for some sort of clue as to who was taking the children from the streets. Now that she was out of the hospital, she could focus. She groaned in frustration. She'd been searching for some sort of lead for hours, but after multiple interviews with people and families, she hadn't turned up a single thought.

"Your Highness?" Kiara looked up in confusion to see two policemen approaching her. Kiara looked behind her, and then to the policemen, who were bowing in front of her. Kiara was confused, "I'm sorry?"

The policemen rose, "Your Highness, if you would come with us." Kiara shook her head, "No, you have the wrong girl…" one of the men smiled, "Princess, do not be afraid. Everything's all right now. Your friends back at the station have a lot to tell you."

Without a question, Kiara hesitantly followed them. She'd been found out. When she entered the station, everyone bowed. "What is this?" she questioned James. He stepped towards her, "I'm a cop. I investigate. When you told me your parents were assassinated and that you were nobility, I was curious. We know who you are, Kiara. You don't have to run anymore. The people who tried to hurt you are locked up in a maximum security prison on the other side of the country. You're safe. You can go home now. Your parents are expecting you." Kiara stepped back, "What? No! I have to stay!"

James laughed, "Kiara, be reasonable. You can't stay on the streets. You're the rightful heir to the throne!" Kiara shook her head, "I revoke my title!" Captain Root stepped forward in alarm, "Kiara, listen. Think about what you're doing." Kiara nodded, "I know. But I'm not right for this country. I revoke my title. Cordelia can have it."

James shook his head, "No, if you revoke your title, it goes to Rowan." Kiara creased her eyebrows in confusion, "Rowan?" James was taken aback, "Yes, Rowan. Do you not know who that is?" Kiara shook her head, "I've never heard that name in my life."

Root and James looked at each other in alarm. "Kiara…" James started nervously, "Rowan is your—"

"I am what?" a voice asked. Kiara turned around to see a boy with dark red curls similar to hers and emerald green eyes standing in the doorway. He was only slightly taller than her, and his eyes held the same look hers always had; a look of mysteriousness and magic.

"Who are you?" she asked. The boy looked at her in the same surprise and said, "Rowan. Who are you?" Kiara's breath quickened, "I'm Kia—Roza." Rowan tilted his head, "Roza?" and without thinking, Kiara put up her hand and tugged his hair slightly.

"Roza," he whispered, "why do I know that name?" Root stood between them and chewed on his toothpick, "You're twins. The king and queen had you separated when you were three. They believed that if you were raised separately and joined back together when you had your powers under control, you wouldn't fight like the last ones and kill everyone again." James looked to Root, "Last ones? Powers?"

Root nodded, "They're the two Faelis. Twins, of all things. You know as well as I do what kind of hysteria people would go into if they knew." Felix scratched his head and interjected, "What's a Faelis?" nearly everyone in the room gasped and turned to him in shock. Felix blushed, "What?"

Kiara sat down next to Rowan, "A Faelis is a magical being. No one knows much about their powers. They're incredibly rare creatures, and there's only two alive at a time. Usually, they never meet. People are afraid of them." Felix shrugged, "How come?"

Rowan looked at Kiara, and then back at Felix. "It happened a long time ago.

"Their names were Faemin and Listow. They were brothers, the first Faelis. When their father discovered that his sons, the princes of Lodos, had these special abilities, he set out to discover their talents and train them as best he could. Each of the sons had different gifts; Faemin was gifted with the power to transform into a wolf, and he was always at battle with himself. He would go from calm and happy to furious in a split second. His power was renowned across the land, and people feared him more than Darkness itself. Listow was the favorite of the two. He was gifted with incredible knowledge and magic. He was calm and free, but stubborn, and refused to move from his views. When their father was on his deathbed, he called his sons to him, and announced that they would share kingship. The two sons were infuriated. Each had wanted to rule alone, for different reasons. It didn't take long after their father's death for them to engage in war against each other. As they each gathered armies, the country split into two. Half was the army of Faemin, who wanted wealth and power, and half was the army of Listow, who wanted equality and prosperity for his people. Families were split; brother fighting brother. It wasn't until they destroyed their own country, their own people, and each other that the war stopped. After that, people started calling these children Faelis, after the two brothers, always a reminder of the evil within them. These children were always outcast and feared, often killed."

Kiara nodded, "We're trademarked by our white hair at birth, which turns dark red when we turn ten. The Light Faelis is characterized by their use of magic, and the Dark by their shapeshifting. People are often more afraid of the Dark Faelis, because they are compelled to be Dark themselves." Felix nodded, "And you're the Dark Faelis?" Kiara nodded, "It's why I was sent to live with wolves as a child. To learn to control myself. I imagine that's why Rowan was also sent away."

Rowan nodded, "I've been learning magic since I was very young. The monks in the desert raised me to live a very peaceful lifestyle, as is my nature." Kiara stood, "This is why I cannot go back. They will never accept me as an heir to the throne as a Dark Faelis. They wouldn't trust me. That's why Rowan should lead the country." Rowan stood up with her, "Wait, wait, wait. I have to lead a country?"

Kiara shrugged, "You're the rightful heir, apparently. Besides, you'd be better than me, trust me. You're only fifteen, anyway. We have another couple years yet."

"Rose, did you want—" Anya came out of the back room and froze when she saw Kiara. Kiara looked at her incredulously, "Anya?" Anya's face was frozen in shock, "Kiara. What are you doing here?" Kiara narrowed her eyes and put her hands to her hips, "I should think you should be the one answering that question." Anya opened her mouth to speak, but only short sounds came out, "I…uh…ah…I um…" Rose looked to Kiara, "She's our medical assistant. She's a complete genius. Why are you so surprised?" Kiara raised her eyebrows, "I should think the reason would be obvious. She's part of the Messengers, she can't be working with you."

Root stepped forward, "She said that she quit. Said she was living with a foster family…who was it? The Chandelles?" Kiara looked to Anya, "Foster family? Is that where you've been spending all your time? In a foster family?" Anya looked to the ground, unsure of what to say.

"What's wrong, Anya?" questioned Kiara angrily, "Am I not family enough for you?" Anya turned on her defensively, "No! But you know I wanted more than what you call home! The Messengers, please! Those kids belong with families who love them, and you know it! I wanted to do this ever since I was little, but you were never going to let me live my dream!" Kiara threw up her hands, "I dragged bodies out of the river for you!" Anya groaned,

"Oh, we both know that you were never going to let me have an actual career with that! I wanted a life, Kiara. A life free from hiding. You were always too caught up with Mother Messenger's antics to care about that, to pay attention. You've always abandoned me for the Messengers!"

"Well, what was I supposed to do? Let you get in all of my fights? I protected you because I knew that I could never, ever forgive myself if anything happened to you. Why do you think I took the blame from Mother Messenger all the time? I wanted to protect you. I've always wanted to protect you."

In her anger, Kiara turned to the rest of the people in the room, "You betrayed me. You called the king and queen. You follow me around, send cops after me. Who do you think you are? Leave me alone! No one must ever know that I am the heir. I am going back to the streets. My duty is to the children first. Keep quiet about this. That's an order." and with only one glance to Rowan, she left the room.

Kiara sighed and leaned against a tree near the lake she had visited earlier. She was so overwhelmed. She needed to focus on the children, not a country.

"I hear you're looking for the stolen children?" a voice said. Kiara looked up, to see James. No, not James. He was slightly taller, and his hair was shorter. His features were sharper, and he had a more relaxed gait.

"Who are you?" she questioned. The man smirked, "The name's Excalibur, and I know who you're looking for." Kiara gave him a suspicious look, "You do?" Excalibur nodded, "A man named Nicodemus. He's been capturing children for months, trying to make an army. He's my older brother. I came to Lodos to try and find a way to stop him." Kiara shook her head, "Why does he want an army of children?" Excalibur shrugged, "Beats me. You're Kiara Santiago, right?" Kiara nodded, and Excalibur full-on smiled, "Queen of the Streets, so I hear. The girl to beat. I also hear you want to rescue the kids."

"How do you know?" Kiara was confused. Excalibur sighed, "Well, when you go knocking door to door, word travels fast." Kiara nodded, "Point taken." and gave him a once-over. This man could be her only link to the children. She had to trust him. "Come with me." she commanded.

Tommy came up to Kiara in a panic, "Kiara," he said, "what *happened* to you? And who's this? Where have you been? Some people came by and said they were friends of yours and that they needed help." Kiara narrowed her eyes, "This is Excalibur, a friend. I wasn't expecting guests. Where are they?" Tommy nodded towards the adjacent room, and went in there to fetch the so called 'friends'.

"Hey, Kiara." Kiara gasped as Holly, Gabriel, Rose, James, Felix, Rowan, and Captain Root came out of the other room. They slowly sauntered in and stood there in a group, surveying the grounds.

"Everyone! Weapons out and behind me!" Kiara was suddenly glad that the entry room was incredibly, incredibly large, for a hundred kids and teenagers came out, dressed entirely in black, with their weapons of choice at the ready. They all stood behind her and handed Kiara her belt and daggers.

"What the—Kiara! What are you doing?" Gabriel cried, "We're your friends!"

"Family comes first!" she yelled, "What are you doing here? How did you get here? How did you know where we were?"

Holly laughed, "You can thank the tracker in your little blondie's bunny. She was put on watch after she tried to run away from the orphanage three times. Though it did take us a while to find out that your hideout was underground. Anya let it slip." Kiara looked at a guilty Anya, who was standing in-between the two groups of people. Eventually, she joined the Messengers' side.

Kiara ignored her and looked down at Linny, "Linny, can I see your bunny?" Linny nodded. Kiara felt around it, and there it was, in the ear. Kiara ripped open the ear just a slit, and took out a pill-sized device. Throwing it on the ground, she crumbled it with my dirty, bare foot. Holly looked at her, "What the hell did you do that for?" Kiara gave her a narrow look as she gave Linny back her bunny, "You have no right to keep tabs on us! Especially not a little girl like Linny!" Captain Root stepped in, "And you have no right to hold them here!"

Kiara went up to him, "I'm not holding them. This is a sanctuary for them. If they want to be here, they can be. If not, that's fine. There's no requirement for them to stay here. We're not doing anything…that illegal. It's what you'd call a…free community." Captain Root gave her his worst look, "Don't you even think about back-talking me." When the others had no words to counter that, the Messengers began to yell in their silence.

"Get out of here!"

"How'd they get in here?"

"Kill 'em!"

Kiara sighed, and then, in her loudest and most fearsome voice, she yelled abruptly, "*Quiet!*" and suddenly, the room was silent. Kiara looked at the group, her eyes sharp and narrowed. No more nice girl. "Members of the L.P.D., you are under arrest for trespassing, breaking and entering, and causing disturbance of the people by the order of the Messengers. Your sentence is one month in the prison cells. You have crossed us for the last time." *I can't have them interfering with me getting those children back.* She looked at Tommy, "Take them down."

Rose looked up at the others, "How long did she say we have to stay in here for?" James, who was reclining against the wall with his eyes closed, replied, "A month." Rose sighed, "Right." James grunted, "It's not so bad. We won't have any food or anything for a while, and it'll be dark like this most of the time. In truth, a month isn't so bad, compared to how mad she was. She could've put us in here for five years. Besides, it isn't so bad. Think of it as...bonding time." he said wryly. The others' heads turned towards him slowly with the 'I-will-kill-you' look. James grimaced and rubbed the back of his neck. "Yeesh," he muttered, "tough crowd."

"I just can't believe we don't even get a fair trial!" Rose continued. Captain Root closed his eyes and did as James had done, "Well, first of all, Kiara's...lair...Kiara's rules. If she doesn't want a trial, she won't get a trial. Second of all, we wouldn't stand a chance in trial. I mean, we were breaking and entering, which is illegal, even in our laws, and we were trespassing on private property without a warrant, which, again, is against our laws. A trial would be a waste of time." Rose sighed, "No, it would buy us time so we could figure out what the hell is up with her." the rest of them shrugged, but Rowan shook his head, "She doesn't want us getting in the way. That's what Anya said. She wants to focus. Right now, all we're doing is hindering her."

Suddenly, the heavy metal door opened, and shut quickly. They could hear distant voices—what sounded like a struggle—and then all was clear. "Dimitri Chandelle, put me down *this instant!*" it was Anya. Then came another voice, "No. Not until you tell me what's going on," and within seconds, a tall young boy carrying Anya passed by and her down in the adjacent cell. "Dimitri, I can't see in here." Anya complained. Dimitri shrugged, "Then I guess you'll just have to trust me. Now seriously, what the hell is going on?" Anya groaned, "It's nothing, I just...I just need to be here right now."

The seven looked at each other, and silently crept up to the small hole in the wall where they could see the moonlit figures of Anya and another boy. Dimitri's hands were on his hips when he spoke. "What, for Kiara? Listen, I don't know what her deal is, but she's not looking out for you anymore. She's forgotten all about you for the last two years! Does she even know you sneak out all the time to see me? You need to be in an environment where you can be cared for and protected." Anya gave Dimitri a glare, "I can take care of myself, Dimitri!" Dimitri gave her the same look back, "I know that, but haven't you ever wanted someone to take care of you for once?" Anya looked to the ground without a reply. Dimitri went closer to her, "Listen, I know you love Kiara. I know you want to help fix her, but you've said it yourself. Sometimes, people are just beyond fixing. I think you have to let her go. She's going to break soon." he brushed a tear away from her eye and whispered, "It's okay to cry, you know. You don't always have to be so strong." Anya swatted his hand away, "Shut up, Dimitri." she said harshly. Dimitri sighed, "Come back." he said, "We all miss you, even Michal. My parents are really worried, and I..." he paused, "I feel like I can't live without you, Anya."

Anya sniffled, "I'm sorry, Dimitri, but I can't. I have to stay here with my sister. It's my duty." Dimitri backed away near the cell door, his face a mask of stone. "Duty means doing things your heart may very well regret." Anya stood up tall and superior, "So be it then." and when Dimitri was about to leave, he stopped and ran back to Anya, hugging her with all his might, "Promise you'll see me again." Anya sniffled, "I promise," and then she broke away, and watched as Dimitri silently left. The gang watched as Anya slowly crumpled to the ground and began to silently cry.

Rose climbed up on a ledge and pushed herself through the hole, falling hard to the cement ground. Anya looked up, "Who's there?" and then Rose wrapped her arms around the little girl, "It's just me, Anya." Anya sniffled and nodded, and then suddenly burst into tears. "What do I do, Rose?" she cried, "What do I do?" Rose sighed, "I don't know," and let Anya cry for a minute on her shoulder. When she was done, she asked, "What are you all doing down here, anyway? You were supposed to be taken to the right wing." Rose shrugged, "This is where they brought us." Anya sighed, "Of course." and silence filled the air.

Without warning, the heavy metal door opened again. Anya and Rose looked at each other, and when they heard two sets of footsteps, they knew it wasn't Dimitri. "Into the next cell!" Anya whispered frantically, "I have to go!" and she pushed Rose through to the other side, and sprinted in the opposite direction.

Kiara and another man who liked like James proceeded into the cell next to them. It must have been the only cell with a door that was broken. They were both

laughing drunkenly. "That was amazing!" Kiara cried
happily. "I can't believe that I have their floor plans now!
This is incredible! You don't know how much of a help this
is! You're the best, Excalibur!" Excalibur shrugged, "I do
my best," and smiled. Then he sat down, "So, Kiara, I was
wondering. I know that Kiara isn't your real name. What is
it?" Kiara looked to the ground, "Roza," she said, "my
name is Roza." Excalibur stood up and put his hand on her
cheek, "It's beautiful," he said, and kissed her other cheek.
Kiara blushed. "So what was it you wanted to ask me?"

"Come with me."

Kiara looked at him strangely, "What do you mean?"
Excalibur grabbed her hands, "Come with me, back to my
home, and together, we can stop my siblings." Kiara raised
an eyebrow, "Just the two of us? Yeah, right." Excalibur
nodded, "Yes. Right. You, with your incredibly amazing
powers and skill, you're our secret weapon. I'm the strategy
and strength. Besides, I know the place like the back of my
hand, and I know everyone's weaknesses. That also means
that I know every secret we could possibly need. We'll be
done within days." Kiara looked to the ground, "But what
about James and Anya and the others?" Excalibur
narrowed his eyes, "What about them? What have they
ever done for you but cause trouble? They follow you all
the time. They never leave you alone. They don't think you
can take care of yourself. They think the Messengers are
bad. All they do is bring you down and hurt you. They
never bring you up." Kiara shrugged, "And what about the

Messengers?" Excalibur shrugged, "It's a few days. Tell them you're going on a personal mission and that Tommy and Anya are in charge. They won't think a thing of it. They're strong, like you." Kiara nodded, "You're right."

Excalibur took her hand and started to walk away. Kiara followed, but suddenly stopped at the door, "But what about James?" she cried, "I can't just leave him!" Excalibur's eyes narrowed again. "What about him? Trust me. I know him way better than you do. All he does is worry about everything. He's always in people's business, and he's always doing something wrong. And remember how he hurt you? Twice? He did it before; don't think he wouldn't do it again just because he's calm now. He's not a good guy, Kiara. You have to remember that." Kiara nodded ruefully, "Let's go." she said, and Excalibur nodded, "We sail at dawn."

—

"TOMMY! ANYA! *TOMMY! ANYA! TOMMY!*" the gang had been yelling all night. It was about two in the morning, hours since Kiara had left, and they'd been desperate ever since. They needed Anya and Tommy to know right away, because James had a secret. Something he wouldn't tell unless they were present.

"*We're coming!*" a furious Anya came stomping down the stairs, with Tommy tailing her, equally angry.

Rose went up to her, "You have to let us out!" she cried. Anya looked her up and down, "What? Why? Kiara specifically gave orders—" Rose cut her off, "You need our help! Let us out! Now! Or you're fired!" In shock, Anya nodded towards the door, and Tommy unlocked it and let them out. "Now," he said, "let's go to the Chambers and see what's up."

The Chambers were a separate set of rooms set off just for private conferences and top-secret plans. Tommy looked around cautiously as he opened the third room, and in they stepped. There was a long table, several chairs, and a wall-length map of Lodos and Alacrast. They all sat down, except for Anya and Tommy, and started asking questions.

"Where did she go?" Anya asked. James nodded to the left, towards the bottom of Alacrast, "That island there. The Black Island. It's where Excalibur's siblings live."

"Who's Excalibur?" Tommy questioned. James sighed, "He's my cousin." Tommy gave him a look, "Elaborate," he commanded, and James obeyed.

"He and his brothers are completely evil. The oldest, Nicodemus, was cursed from birth, or so he claims. No one's ever even seen him without his red cloak. Lucius is an evil genius. He's about as smart as Anya, and he's cunning. Very cunning. Calvin and Excalibur are twins. They're attractive and strong and they use that to lure people to trust them. They're very persuasive but they're not completely screwed up. I remember having fun with them as kids."

Anya sighed, "Right. Okay. So what does he want with Kiara?" James groaned, "Oh, come, on, Anya, you're smarter than that! She's one of the two Faelis! One of those, and he'll be invincible. If Excalibur persuades Kiara to train and learn everything and use her Dark power—whatever that may be—for their cause, we're plain out screwed. Lodos is screwed. This is a lot bigger than just Kiara. This involves everyone."

Anya nodded, "Then we need to get down there and stop this. Now." James nodded, "I know where they're leaving from. I heard it while they were leaving." Tommy ran to the other side of the room, "Then let's go."

"Come on, hurry up! We'll miss them!" Anya and Tommy were ahead of them all. By the time they reached the pier, it took the others ten more seconds to catch up with them.

"Oh, no," Anya whispered into the wind. There was a ship that had already set sail, with a red-haired girl facing them. Anya went to the very edge, "Kiara!" she cried, "Kiara, come back!" Kiara glared at her, "No!" she shouted.

James went up there with Rose. "Come on, Kiara, please!" Rose was crying now. Kiara said nothing. James groaned, "Kiara! Come back!" and Excalibur came around and stood behind her, "Not gonna happen, James." James growled, "Kiara, this isn't funny!" Kiara raised her eyebrows, "And it looks like I'm laughing?"

"Kiara!" he cried. They were getting farther and farther away. Soon they would be but a dot in the distance. Kiara rolled her eyes, turned around, and walked away.

"Kiara..." James whispered. Felix and Gabriel looked at him, "We'll get her back, man," Gabriel said, "Don't you worry."

CHAPTER 6:

"Left! Now right! Don't forget that lower leg! Again! Left! Right! Solid!" Excalibur chanted the words over and over in the training room to his two newest trainees. They were exceptional; completely exceptional, and he could not have been more pleased with himself. He had both Faelis completely within his control, now that Rowan had tried to save his sister and failed. He would be unstoppable now to help his siblings take control of the two countries.

After another rep and set of defense and attack strategies, he had mercy, "You are dismissed!" he'd spend six long hours with them simply training. Not to mention planning, strategizing, conditioning, techniques, et cetera. He was tired, and so were they. Besides, he couldn't have them completely worn out. Then what good would they be? He needed them as fit and alert as possible at all times. There was no telling what would happen on this island. Without even a glance back, he left the sparring room, and went off to his secret study.

"Come on, Kiara, let's go." called Rowan from the other side of the room. He was no good at fighting. He knew it. His bruises and scrapes only further proved that his brains were better than his brawn. Kiara nodded, feeling only a twinge of guilt for taking out her full force on him. It seemed to spike more and more each day she was here, her anger. And she took it out on anything when she had the chance, which, lately, was her brother. Kiara sighed, resolved to make it up to him, picked up her daggers, and the two of them headed up the very long, very high staircases to their rooms.

"I'm going to go polish these," Kiara said distractedly as she picked at her daggers. Rowan gave her one last look of exhaustion, "Okay. I'll be in the middle room." Neither of them really used their separate bedrooms unless there was a serious fight. They shared a common room, and stayed close together. They didn't mind for the most part, and it felt better not to be so isolated when such dark thoughts and energy surrounded them. Kiara nodded her head, and walked the opposite way to the washroom, firstly proceeding to wipe the sweat, dirt, and grime off of her precious and prized daggers. They were beautiful, pure silver, each of them encrusted with a single emerald, to symbolize her strange emerald eyes. They were her mother's, the only thing that she had left of her.

Her mother. Kiara could faintly remember her rich brown hair and bright green eyes. A deep, sweet voice cooing melodies for her to sleep to, and a bubbly laugh. The sweet scents of grass and parchment.

"Ah! Damn!" Kiara, lost in her faraway daydream, had let the knife she was polishing slip out of her grip and slice a long, deep cut down her right palm. "Damn it," she muttered under her breath as she put the knife down and ran cold water onto her hand to stop the bleeding. *Red blood. Red like the blood you've spilt. Red for anger. Red for betrayal. Red like the hair upon your head.* Kiara sighed and mentally slapped herself, *Stop thinking in riddles. You're insane enough as it is.* She sighed and looked down at her newly clotted wound, thankful that it had stopped bleeding. Without thinking, she looked up into the mirror.

At first, she didn't recognize her reflection, and was shocked when she came to realize that the frightening figure in the mirror was herself. Her hair was greasy, matted, and dull, leaving back a dull brick red instead of the beautiful brilliant red tresses she'd once possessed. Her skin was sallow and pale; she could almost see the veins along her cheekbones and temple and hairline; her scars were more prominent than ever, especially the scar that ran diagonally across her face. Her face was thin and bony, the flesh was all but wasted away, and her collarbone was scarily visible beneath her thin, sheer shirt. Her eyes were dull and lifeless, barely green, and certainly not the emerald that used to define her. *What happened to me? Is this a nightmare?* But Kiara knew that it was reality. Of course it was. What did she expect? She hadn't bathed in a time frame that shouldn't be real. She didn't own a brush for her hair, and she'd eaten little and had worked off much more than she'd eaten. It had just been so long since she'd looked in a mirror. Her reflection wasn't just startling because of her appearance, but also of the illusion of her age.

Quietly, Kiara washed off her daggers carefully without looking again in the mirror, put them in their sheath, and quietly went back to her shared room. As she walked in, trying to look as though nothing had happened, she saw her brother sitting at the window-bench with a photograph of a girl in his hands. He was gazing at her fondly with an almost sorrowful expression on his face, something that you could not describe simply. "Again?" Kiara questioned. Startled by her sudden entrance, Rowan nearly dropped the picture. He looked at her and shrugged, "She's always on my mind. I might even love her." Kiara sighed, "And why would you think that?" Rowan shrugged, "I don't know. I can't help but think about her. I smile endlessly when I am around her. I want to make her happy, do everything I can for her. I want to kiss her, I want to hold her in my arms and never let her go. I want to be with her for the rest of my life. I want—" Kiara shook her head and cut him off, "Who is she, anyway, lover boy? And how exactly do you know each other?" a dreamy look overcame Rowan's face, "We met at school. She was an exchange student from Raiki. Her name's Layna. When she was having trouble keeping up, her guardians hired me to be her tutor. We've never stopped seeing each other since."

Kiara nodded, "And where is she now?" Rowan sighed, "I don't know. I haven't heard from her since we came here. I'm beginning to worry that she'll think I've left her." Kiara shrugged and rolled her eyes, "Well, we need to focus anyway. We have a very important mission in six months. We can't stop now. If anything, we need to work harder." Rowan laughed, "You're just a slave driver, aren't you?" Kiara rolled her eyes and put her daggers in her drawer, pausing to look at the worn-out letter that she used to read daily. "What's that?" asked Rowan. Kiara quickly shut the drawer, "Nothing." she said, and laid down on her bed, her eyes closed. Rowan looked at her, then stood up, walked over to the vanity, and opened the drawer. Kiara' eyes snapped open, "Hey! Get out of there!" but Rowan already had the letter in his hand. "And what is this?" he asked charismatically. Kiara' cheeks flamed red, "Give that back!" she cried, but Rowan held it out of her grasp. "A letter? From who? Who are *you* seeing?"

"I'm not seeing anyone! Now give it back!" Rowan shook his head, "Well, who's it from, then?" Kiara looked daggers at him, "No one!" Rowan raised an eyebrow, "Oh, really? Because the only way you'd have this is if someone would have given it to you. And looking at the *J* on the back, I'm pretty sure it isn't from Garren. Who gave it to you?" Kiara stomped on the floor, "Who cares? Give it back!" Rowan shook his head again, "No. Not until you tell me who it's from." Kiara sighed in defeat, "A friend," she mumbled. Rowan nodded, "What friend?" Kiara looked down to the ground, "James," she said, and Rowan nodded, "James? You mean that boy from the police station? Isn't he supposed to be your mortal enemy or something? From what you've described of him, at least." Kiara sat down on her bed, "Yes. James. It's from him." Rowan looked at her, "What does it say?" when he received no reply, he pressed on, "Well? What does it say? If you don't tell me, I'll read it myself!" but Kiara shrugged, "Go ahead. It's nothing, anyway. It means nothing." Rowan gave a small shrug, "Suit yourself."

Rowan opened the letter, and began to read. Only a few sentences in, and already he was intrigued. He hadn't heard much of the James boy, and what he had heard hadn't exactly been condoling. But when he read this letter through, it was as if this was a totally different person, a different facade, or at least the part of him Kiara had said nothing about. When he was finished with the letter, Rowan read the last line about ten times, making sure his eyes hadn't deceived him.

I think I love you.

"You call this nothing? This? Really? How can you call this nothing?" he was yelling at her. Kiara looked up and glared at him, "Because it's not. It never was." Rowan waved the letter in his sister's face, "How can you say it wasn't? When a man says he loves you, he means it! What *really* happened, Kiara?" Kiara looked at him, "Nothing. And it doesn't matter, anyway." Rowan looked at her, his eyes ablaze, "Doesn't matter? *Doesn't matter?* A man has just confessed to you that he *loves* you, Roza! How does that not matter?" Kiara groaned, "Oh, he doesn't love me!" Rowan raised his eyebrows, "And what, pray tell, would give you *that* sign?" Kiara narrowed her eyes, "Do you know how many times he's betrayed me? He said he *thinks.* He doesn't know! I'd rather not know! I've been tortured enough."

"Oh, you don't know torture, Roza!" he knew that his bold statement would render the truth out of her, and he was right. It did.

"Torture? How *dare* you say that I don't know torture? I know torture more than you'll ever know! I won't go into the details of our tragic past, but I have gone through more pain that any human should ever have to go through! Don't ever say that I don't know torture!" a tear ran down Kiara' face as she took back the letter, crumpled it up, and threw it into the fireplace.

"Hey!" Rowan cried as he pulled the singed paper out of the embers. Kiara was already out of the room, so he made sure that no severe damage had been done, and put it in his drawer, smiling sadly. *Finally, some emotion out of her.*

—

Later that night, there were two knocks, and then, with a strong gust of wind, the heavy double doors slammed open. In walked five imposing figures, all of them men. There was a younger one with black hair, and whose face was as menacing as his demeanor, a slightly older one with long, sleek blonde hair that was greased back, Excalibur, and then a man in a black cloak, who was the tallest of them all. The man in the cloak walked up to them.

"Roza Collins," he said in a low growl, his red eyes piercing out from underneath the cloak, "we hear you plan to betray us." Rowan walked forward in her defense, "Of course not," he said, "why would you think—" the man swiped his long, clawed hand, to his right, sending Rowan across the room. "Rowan!" Kiara cried, and glared daggers at the cloaked man, "Leave him alone, Nicodemus! He did nothing!" Nicodemus turned his attention towards her, "Well, if you don't plan to betray us, then you won't mind spending your time in the cells." Kiara lifted her chin, "Why?" Excalibur stepped forward, "We need to test your mental breaking point. Solitary confinement is the best possible option. Guys?"

The two other men went over to Kiara and grabbed her. Excalibur sped over to Rowan and held him back with difficulty, "Watch your place, Faelis!" Kiara screamed and kicked as she was dragged away, "Rowan!" Rowan tried his best to escape, but it was no use, "She's done nothing wrong!" he cried, but Excalibur only tightened his grip, "It doesn't matter. They don't care. She'll be fine, Faelis." Rowan watched as his sister was dragged out of the room, and Excalibur finally let him go. Rowan let a tear fall down his face, "What have you done to her?" Excalibur looked confused, "Done to her? I'm afraid I don't know what you mean." Rowan turned on him with all the fury of his sister, "That is not Roza! I know my sister! What have you *done* to her?" Excalibur pondered this for a second, and just before leaving the room, glanced back, "You knew her for three years. Maybe this is how she really is. Perhaps it isn't even what I've done to her, but what she's done to herself."

Rowan stood there for a few moments, and then slowly made his way to his sister's side of the room. He opened her drawer, and pulled out her daggers and her letter. "Oh, Roza..." he whispered to himself. He slipped the letter and daggers in his satchel. "I'll fight for you." he promised her.

—

Rowan kicked the dummy in frustration. It had been five days since Kiara had been taken down to the prison. He knew he couldn't break her out; Excalibur and the others would find out, and it'd be too obvious. Besides, where would they go? They had no idea where they were. It was impossible, and Rowan couldn't use his transportation spell. There was a magic barrier over the castle, and who knew how far the barrier reached? If it reached for miles, they wouldn't stand a chance. He grunted with fury and struck the dummy again. He couldn't keep racking his brains out like this. He had to do something. But what?

With a sudden idea, he left the practice room and tore down the hall, skidding into his room. He grabbed a piece of paper and a pen, and began to write. When he was done, he went to the window and whistled to summon his owl, Bane. He tied the letter around the owl's foot, "Anya." he said, and with a nudge, away the owl went.

Now all he could do was wait.

—

Anya woke up to screeching and scratching on the door of the police complex. She'd fallen asleep at her desk again. These late nights were killing her. She sat up and looked at the door, and stood up suddenly. An owl? What was an owl doing out in the morning? It must be sick. Wait, what was that on its foot? Anya opened the door, and the owl landed on her outstretched arm. Anya untied the piece of paper around his foot and opened the small scroll.

Need help. We're in trouble. The owl will lead you here. Rowan.

With wide eyes, Anya let the owl go, and called to James, Root, Holly, Gabriel, Rose, and Felix in the back room, "Guys!" she cried, "We're going on a road trip!"

—

Rowan grunted as he pulled up the rope, pulling in Anya from the window. He looked to the gang, "I can't thank you enough for coming." Anya took his hand, "She's my sister and our friend, whether we'd like to admit it or not. We'd do anything for her." Rowan nodded, "Okay, she's in the dungeon. They said it's some kind of…breaking point exercise, but if that were true, they'd be putting me down there, too. Chances are that they know she was planning secretly to get out of here. I put a spell on myself so that they can't figure out with Raiu's magic what's going on in my head, but Ro would never let me put a spell on her."

James nodded, "Typical. Alright, so what's our plan of attack?" Rowan ushered them all silently down the stairs, "We need to get to the dungeon using my invisibility spell. Once there, we find a way to break her out, and get out of here. Somehow." Root shrugged, "It's better than nothing. Let's go."

The dungeon was dark and damp. It's musty, thick smell made it obvious it hadn't been used in quite a long time. They heard humming, and followed it to a single lit torch, right across from a cell. They clambered over to the cell, where Kiara had gotten up defensively at the sound of the footsteps, "What do you want now?" she cried.

Rowan ran to the bars, "Ro, Ro, it's us! It's just us. We're here to get you out." Kiara looked more closely at the figures behind him, "How did you guys get here?" Rowan shook his head, "Never mind that. James, Gabriel, come on, help me bust these rusty bars open." James and Gabriel nodded, and with all their might, they pulled on the rusty old bars until a bolt gave out, and then another, and then another, until the gate was almost completely unhinged. Kiara climbed out of the cell and nodded, "I know how to get out of here."

Kiara led them down a dark tunnel. "How can you see in here?" Anya asked incredulously. Kiara shrugged, "I don't. I feel what's around me. I've been down here countless times, trying to get the layout of the place memorized. There's a bend around here, and then there's a drop-off." Root, Rose, Gabriel, Anya, James, Felix, and Rowan stopped simultaneously, "What are we supposed to do after we hit that?" James cried. Kiara glared daggers at him, "Shh! We're going to climb down. It's a rock wall, it's not rocket science. You'll survive. Probably."

The others looked at one another, but reluctantly followed Kiara, who, after about another ten minutes of walking, sighed. "Well, here it is. Let's climb." she turned around and proceeded to climb down the rock wall as though it were a ladder. Anya and Rowan went next, their deft and quick limbs proving to be fit perfectly for this job. Holly and Root grabbed hands and went together, Felix and Gabriel gave each other a nod as if to say, *Nice knowing you,* and went down, and finally, James proceeded to descend the treacherous rock wall with Rose.

"You guys all right?" Kiara cried from the bottom. Anya and Rowan grunted as they jumped a foot to the bottom and nodded. Holly and Root didn't answer in an effort to concentrate on what they were doing. Felix and Gabriel gave slightly noticeable nods, and James called down, "Yeah!" as he helped Rose.

When they had all reached the bottom safely, Kiara nodded, "Rowan, work your magic." Rowan smiled mischievously and closed his eyes to focus. In moments, they were all back at the police station.

Root and Holly looked at them incredulously, "You couldn't do that anyway? Inside the building? Months ago?" Rowan shook his head, "There was a magic guard on the whole castle. I didn't even know about the tunnel until today." Heads turned to Kiara, who shrugged, "I wasn't going to go until I had a solid plan. Nicodemus and the others foiled that plan when they put me in the dungeon."

Rose sighed and sat down, "So what now?" Rowan looked to Kiara, who sighed. "It's time to put things right. Rowan needs to take the crown. I need to pay for my crimes. I know what I've done, so arrest me." James stepped forward, "But what about the kids?" Kiara shook her head, "That's for Anya now. It's your guys' job to take care of Nicodemus now that you know where to look." Gabriel sat down, "But these people are forces that we can't deal with on our own." Root held a hand up, "Yes, we can. Kiara is right. She finally got some sense in her."

Kiara stuck out her arms, "So here I am. Arrest me. Do what you've been trying for years to do." Captain Root and Holly were speechless along with the rest of them. But unlike the others, they weren't overcome and frozen with shock. They tentatively stood up and walked over to Kiara, cuffing her as they repeated, "Kiara Santiago, you are under arrest for the murder and robberies of the citizens of the Capital and other known cities of Lodos. You have the right to remain silent, and anything you say can and will be used in a court of law. You have the right to an attorney. If you cannot afford one, the court will assign one to you." Kiara laughed, "Attorney? I wave that right. No attorney could make me look innocent." Holly and Captain Root looked at her and shrugged, "Whatever you say," they said, and led her away.

—

"What is your name?" Kiara sighed, "Kiara Santiago." Captain Root looked at her with an exhausted glance, "No, Kiara. Your real name."

"My full name?"

"Yes."

"With title?"

"If you please."

"Princess Roza Kiara Collins." Captain Root nodded, "Continuing. What is your date of birth?"

"You already know that." He sighed, "I know, but it's procedure. Just do it, will you?"

And so the questioning continued.

"Come on, Rose, we've got to go! We can't be late for her trial!" James yelled up the stairs. He'd been waiting for fifteen minutes now. They were going to be late!

"Rose!" He called again, more urgently.

"What?" James turned around abruptly, and there was Rose, dressed beautifully in a dusty-rose colored summer dress and practical nursing shoes. "What are you yelling about? Come on! Let's go! We're going to be late!" James shook his head and sighed, "Okay. Everyone else is waiting there for us." Rose nodded, "Okay. I hope this goes well." James gave her a quick hug, "It will."

It has to.

—

"I call Ms. Kiara Santiago to the stand!" called the prosecutor. Kiara stood up and walked over to the booth, where she made an oath to tell the truth, the whole truth, and nothing but the truth, and sat down.

"Now, Ms. Santiago, how old are you?" Kiara shrugged, "Fifteen." the woman nodded, "And I understand that you're the number one most wanted on just about every criminal justice organization's list?" Kiara nodded, "You've understood." the woman gave her a questionable look, "What would you say caused your crimes?" Kiara gave her the same look, "I'm not sure I understand the question." the woman shrugged, "Okay, well, I'll put it this way. Why did you commit your crimes? Your murders, in specifics?" Kiara sighed and thought for a second before answering. "Well, at first, it was for the Messengers. We had tasks to do, and if we didn't do them, we'd be punished."

"What kind of punishment would you receive if you didn't finish these so-called tasks?"

"Well, it depends on the crime you didn't commit or messed up. For my tasks in particular, I would have been whipped. Chinese water torture was also an option." the woman raised her eyebrows, "How old were you when you joined the Messengers?"

"It was five months after my tenth birthday." the woman nodded again, "And what about after the Messengers? What caused you to kill then?" Kiara gave her an odd look, like she was daydreaming. "Well, the person probably threatened me, or Anya. Or they got in the way, they were dangerous to me and Anya, or they had something we needed. If you're asking if I killed the innocent without a plausible reason, the answer to that is never." the woman nodded, "And your robberies? What about them?"

"Again, for the Messengers, but before and after that, it was for survival. Food mostly. Sometimes things to wash our hair or brush our teeth. Other times, we needed clothes. We took things from second-hand stores, where there usually weren't cameras or security systems. And we took money, too, but not as often. We used the money to buy food and things. We didn't always steal." the woman nodded, "So you're saying that your crimes were acts of survival?" Kiara shrugged, "Only some of them. The ones for the Messengers were in cold blood, and some of the murders after that were, too. Some." the woman nodded, "That is all."

A man, whom she assumed was her court-appointed lawyer or attorney that James had probably insisted they give her, stood up and addressed her, "Now, Ms. Santiago, you mentioned a 'before' the Messengers. What was before, and how did you come to be in the Messengers?"

"That, sir, I'm afraid is a rather long story." the man looked around, "Well, we have time. Judge?" Kiara looked at the Judge, who nodded, "Go on, Ms. Santiago." Kiara rolled her eyes, "Jacob, just call me Kiara." the courtroom gasped, and Kiara rolled her eyes again, "Jeez, you people." she sighed, "When I was little, I was a princess. Seventh princess of Lodos, Roza. The wolf girl. Everyone knew *of* me, but no one actually knew me. On my tenth birthday, there was a ball, where masked strangers tried to assassinate me. Anya and I were told to run away, so we did, and wandered around for a month, scavenging. We were taken in by an orphanage, but they tried to separate us, so we ran away from there. One day, we were sitting in a bare alleyway. Some young boy, Tommy, came up to us and offered us food and shelter. Said he was a street kid like us. We followed him, and were no sooner Mother Messenger's favorites." the man nodded, "Sounds like a tragedy. You mentioned your sister quite a bit. Tell me, was she with you in your crimes?" Kiara's eyes narrowed, "She was always with me, wherever I went. But she only did things under Mother Messenger's or my orders. Leave her alone." the man raised his hands, "Of course. Just clarifying. No further questions."

Judge Abernathy nodded, "Closing arguments. The people's argument?" the woman stood up, "As you can plainly see, this young woman is a cold-blooded criminal. She can't be trusted; we've seen what she's capable of…" Kiara snorted. No, they hadn't. How long would this lady keep jabbering away? Blah, blah, blah, she's a bad person, blah, blah, blah she needs to be stopped. Kiara had heard it a thousand times before. She sighed in relief when the lady was done, and the man stood up to present his argument.

Just as Kiara had thought, here came the sob story. How poor princesses Roza and Anastasia had been practically forced to leave their home and their families because of attempted assassination, and had gone downhill from there. It wasn't her fault that she was violent; it wasn't her fault of the crimes she'd committed; she'd been forced to do them. She had to, to ensure their welfare and survival. Yeah, yeah. She'd heard that one before, too. The funny thing was, neither of them were true.

"If that is all, I call a fifteen-minute recess for the jury to decide their verdict." the mallet slammed down, and the people left.

Kiara looked at the guard, "I need to talk to my friends. Last words, you know?" when the guy gave her a wary look, she rolled her eyes, "I'm not going to do anything. I handed myself in, remember? And if I was going to do something, don't you think I'd have done it already?" shrugging, the guard gestured for her to get lost.

Kiara made her way out of the courtroom and down the hallway. James looked up as she approached him. "Kiara!" James stood up abruptly, not sure if he was supposed to be thrilled or angry.

Finally, he settled on angry. "What do you want?" he asked sharply. Kiara's body language told him that she didn't care what he said or how he said it. That she was numb and cold inside, like she always had been. But her eyes told a different story. She was desperate for him to help her; she needed someone's shoulders to lean on.

"I came to say goodbye. We all know what the jury's going to decide." James nodded, "Well, goodbye, then, Kiara Santiago. It was a pleasure knowing you." Kiara nodded, "Likewise." James held out his hand, and Kiara placed her shaky one in his. They shook, and turned away from each other.

Just as Kiara was about to enter the courtroom again, she felt a hand grab her wrist. She looked up. James. He looked at her, and she could almost see the tears forming in his eyes. When the judge pounded his mallet once again, she pulled away from his grasp. "Goodbye, James." and went to stand beside the man who was representing her.

"On the uncounted amounts of murder in the first degree, how do find the defendant?" one of the jury members stood up, with cards in his hands, "We find the defendant guilty, Your Honor." Kiara leaned towards her representative, "Aren't they actually supposed to count these things?" the attorney shrugged, "You're a special case." Kiara nodded, "Of course I am." The judge slammed his mallet, bringing Kiara back to reality. "On the uncounted amounts of burglary in the first degree, how do you find the defendant?" again, the man said, "We find the defendant guilty, Your Honor." the judge slammed his mallet again, "On the uncounted amounts of assault in the first degree, how do you find the defendant?" the man answered one last time, "We find the defendant guilty, Your Honor." the judge didn't bother to slam his mallet. "I hereby order the defendant, Kiara Santiago, to immediate death. Court is adjourned." he slammed his mallet, and Kiara was led away to the last place she would see.

James stood up and was about to cry out, but when he saw Rose's face, he decided against it. They were both in pain; and they would both do what Kiara wanted them to. Be silent.

Kiara let herself be led to a concrete room. There, the guard left her in the hands of a young man in a doctor's suit, along with his small assistant. Kiara sat down in the chair, and when the heavy metal door clashed shut, the doctor and assistant pulled off their masks.

Anya and Tommy gave her sly smiles, and she returned the glance. After slipping out of her cuffs, she looked up at the window, "So that's where I go out? And how do I stay out of sight?" Anya snorted, and Tommy laughed. "You're Kiara Santiago. You'll be just fine." Kiara nodded, "Good. And you two will meet me at headquarters? I assume you told no one?" they both nodded, "Good. The Messengers are in for a surprise. Now, Anya, you've made a duplicate, right?" Anya nodded, "It will be good for five years. Tangible and all. It just will be…dead. Well, the illusion of dead. And they won't bury you. You've donated your body to science." Kiara nodded, "I always thought I'd need an education. Now, you two, I'll see you tomorrow." they nodded, "Thanks for this," she said, and they both laughed, "What? Helping out with the biggest scam in fifty years? Thank *you!*" Kiara sighed and laughed, looking up at the window. "Well, see you." and was about to go, when Tommy stopped her. "Hey, James gave this to one of the guards and they gave it to me. It's for you." Kiara nodded, took the letter, and out she went, running silently and unseen through her disguise towards the Messenger headquarters.

It's not over yet.

CHAPTER 7:

Dear Kiara,

Okay. I know that's a crappy beginning, but I couldn't think of anything else to say.

Truthfully, I don't even know what to say right now. I'm stunned, speechless, in shock. I mean, we all knew what the verdict would be, like you said, but I never really imagined it as a reality. I kept thinking—hoping—that you would pull one of your last-minute stunts and magically escape, like you had so many times before.

I know our last words were…tense…and there's no one to blame there. You were trying to do what you thought was right, and I was just trying to do that, too. But you know that. I just wanted to say…I'm sorry. And I hope you can forgive me for earlier.

The locket in the envelope is yours. Keep it.

Yours forever,

James

Kiara looked up from the worn out sheet of paper, fiddling with the locket that had been enclosed in the envelope, to the blank, brown clay walls that made up the Catacombs, or living areas, of the Messenger headquarters. She'd read that letter a thousand times over in the last two years, ever since her fake death. It got harder and harder every time not to cry out in pain every time she read it, but she kept herself together and told herself what she'd been telling herself for years. Crying is a sign of weakness. So don't cry. Don't scream. Don't yell. Keep it together. Let no one see what's going on inside.

Anya had grown into that sort of mode, too. Kiara guessed being around her really made it hard for Anya to express herself the way she used to. She used to say everything she thought, everything that was needed to be said. She spoke her thoughts and feelings, and if she was sad, she cried. If she was angry, she yelled. If she was scared, she screamed. But through the last couple years, she'd finally succumbed to the Messenger ways and had given up on expressing. Kiara made her lose her first love, her first best friend, the first family that didn't judge her. She'd destroyed all of that, and she felt terrible, but what was done was done. Besides, Kiara couldn't take the chance that they might throw her in an orphanage, or even worse, send her to prison like Kiara sent herself. She couldn't let her repeat her mistakes.

"Hey," Kiara looked up, surprised. Tommy was standing in the doorway of her room. She nodded, "Hey." Tommy saw the folded-up, dirt-and-blood-stained letter in her hand, and sighed, "Kiara," he sat down next to her, "you can't keep going on like this. You're dead to them now, literally. You have to go on with your life. You can't keep hanging on to the past. You have to let them go." Kiara nodded, "Yeah, I know, Tommy. I know." He patted her shoulder, "Come on. We'd probably better get going. You've got the convention tonight, and Anya's freaking out because she can't find you. If you don't hurry, everyone will have permanent hand marks on their faces." Kiara chuckled a little, "Yeah. Okay, I'll go find her." Tommy winked at her, "Go get 'em."

Kiara sighed, put the letter in the pocket of her uniform, and went out to Anya, "So, Anya, what do we do today?" Anya shrugged, "Not much. No recent activity, no Sensor reports, nothing. For now, they lie dormant." Kiara sighed again and nodded, "Right." and then Tommy spoke up, "Hey, Anya, what's that? It looks like six little dots...oh no!" Tommy pushed Kiara into a small little hovel and whispered, "Keep quiet! Messengers! To your stations! It's the L.P.D.!" Kiara gasped. The L.P.D.? What were they doing here? And more importantly, how had they found them again? They'd moved! And what did they want?

"Get them!" Kiara heard Tommy shout. She peeked out of the hovel; they had the gang: James, Gabriel, Rose, Felix, Holly, and Captain Root, tied up in the middle of the room.

"What are you doing here?" Tommy asked fiercely. Captain Root sighed, "Look, we—"

"How did you get here?"

"We saw the sewer lid was off, and we went to investigate. Convenient, really."

"What do you want?"

"Well, if you'd let me finish a sentence, I could tell you." Tommy sighed, and with the nod from Anya, Tommy shut up. Captain Root sighed, "We came to return something to you." Tommy had a confused look on his face, "What do you mean?" Captain Root sighed, "In my pocket. There's a few letters." Tommy dug into Root's pocket and pulled out a few letters.

"It was Kiara's," he said. "We know how much she meant to all of you, so that's why we're not trying to arrest any of you. We know how she'd react, and that's the last thing we want her to feel down in the Underworld where we all know she's having a hell of a time. These are her last words to James, and there's another one, to you and Anya and the rest of the Messengers." Kiara cringed. Tommy knew about the letter to them, it had been to make the scheme more believable. But they'd found her letter to James? This could not be good.

"James? What did the letter to James say?" Kiara could feel Tommy's glare at her from his stance in the middle of the room, even though it was only psychological. She wasn't supposed to have replied to him, but she did anyway. Kiara never gave it to him, she actually left it in the branches of a tree out in the orchard beside his house. She never thought he would find it, though she secretly hoped he would.

Captain Root cleared his throat:

"James,

I know. It's an even worse beginning than yours. I couldn't think of anything else to say, though. Words just seem to escape me right now.

Listen, James, about your letter. I forgive you. It's fine. But I want you to forget about me. Please. Go on with your life, the way it was before you met me. You'll be much better off that way, believe me.

Goodbye.

Kiara"

Tommy sighed, "So what—"

"Kiara! Kiara! Come here, quick! Quick! Lily's hurt!" *No!* Kiara looked at James and the gang's expressions as their faces became shocked and confused, even more so when Linny came running into the room, holding her bunny sloppily in her arms.

Tommy cleared his throat nervously, "Um, Linny…Kiara isn't here. Remember?" he was hoping that she would catch on and keep quiet, but Kiara knew what would happen. Linny was not good at keeping secrets.

She looked up at Tommy, genuinely confused, "What? But I saw her in the little hole in the wall." Linny came over to Kiara and dragged her out, "Kiara, come on!" Kiara looked at the gang. They were shocked, stunned, literally speechless, and they were all as pale as death. She could see Rose's mouth shaking, tears spilling down her cheeks, and James, whose expression was the worst of them all—unreadable. Linny tugged on her hand, and she looked to her left as one of the Messengers brought Lily, Linny's dog, into the room. Kiara took Lily and looked at her paw, where she'd cut it.

"I need bandages and disinfectant." and within moments, the materials were brought to her. In silence, she put disinfectant on the cut and wrapped it firmly with bandages. She gave Lily to Linny and said, "Now go back to the playroom. And be careful with her foot." Linny nodded and ran off. Kiara stood up, all eyes on her, and looked at Tommy, "Untie them." she said.

Tommy looked at her, "But, Kiara—" she held up a hand, "Untie them. Now. And bring them down to the ballroom. No one else is allowed in, am I clear?" with reluctance, Tommy nodded, and Kiara went up to the balcony, where she'd made her own personal space. She sighed and started fiddling with her locket, the one that James had given her. She was nervous; very nervous, but she was also very happy, and relieved. Just like when she'd first ran away, she had been wrong about her scheme. It was hard; harder than she'd imagined. She'd made a resolution to think things through emotionally and mentally as well from now on.

"Where is she?" Kiara heard Rose, frantic. Kiara sighed, closed her eyes, and stood up. "I'm here." Rose turned around, and gasped as she saw her descending the stairs. Kiara could see her tear-streaked face, and it broke her heart. She hadn't meant to make her that sad; she hadn't meant to make anyone that sad.

"…Kiara?" she asked in a small voice. Kiara nodded and reached the bottom floor, "Hi, Rose." Kiara's voice was as small as Rose's. Without warning, Kiara was crushed in her fierce embrace, Rose's sobs shattering her soul. Kiara hugged her back just as fiercely, enjoying the warmth of her body. She felt like the half of herself that had been gone had been replaced. Rose pulled away and looked at Kiara, her face suddenly angry.

"Why?" she cried, and boy, was she angry, "Why did you do this? Do you know how torn I've been? Do you know what I've been going through? All of us? How could you?" Kiara sighed, "Rose, I'll explain that in a moment. Please, everyone, have a seat." Kiara sat opposite of them and fiddled with her locket silently. She knew they would have questions, many of them.

"Let's just get this over with. I know you must have a lot of questions." Kiara sighed, and looked at Holly. She shrugged, "How are you alive?" Kiara laughed a little. "Well, it's really very easy. The doctor and nurse who were supposed to put the needle in my arm were tied up by Tommy and Anya, who posed as the doctor and nurse themselves. They helped me escape from the skylight. I ran, and here I am." She looked to Captain Root, and he sighed, "Why did you do it?" I shrugged, "I'm planning something large. Nothing to do with crime or the city. It's something…personal, let's say. And I couldn't deal with that and everything else in my life. So I dropped my life so I could focus. It's what you wanted, anyway, isn't it? Me dead? I gave everyone what they wanted, and I got what I needed. Win-win situation." Captain Root nodded. He understood, but he didn't think that it was entirely true.

Kiara looked at Gabriel and Felix, and they shook their heads. No questions, so she turned to Rose. She had an upset expression, and Kiara didn't blame her a bit. "Did you ever stop to think about us? About how we would feel?" Kiara sighed, "Truthfully, no. I didn't think that any of you, except you, would care. I mean, Holly and Captain Root brought me to court, this was what they wanted. Felix and Gabriel don't know me that well, and James and I met because he wanted to take me to his brother to be executed. Besides you, I didn't think anyone would care. But I thought you'd understand. I thought you'd come up with some rational explanation." Rose sniffled and shook her head without saying a word.

Kiara looked at James, but he wouldn't look at her. She sighed, cleared her throat, and headed up the stairs, "Well, this has been…awkward. Now, if you all don't mind, I'm quite busy. Please, no one must know I'm alive, and no one must know where we are. Thank you for visiting. If you please, forget this happened." without another word, she left and went into the storage room to grab something for Anya. She heard hushed whispers, scuffling feet, and then, "Wait!" it was James, "Wait, Kiara, wait!" he ran up the stairs and stopped behind her, "Kiara, please, wait." Kiara sighed, turned around, and looked at him, "What?" she asked. He was breathing heavily and was struggling to find the right words.

"Kiara…" he paused, still not knowing what to say. Kiara shrugged, "James, let it go. Let me go. I don't belong in your life. I don't belong in any of your lives. Just...let me be. It's easier that way." She sighed and began to walk further into the room. She heard him grunt and race towards her, and before she had time to react, he caught her wrist and swung her around.

"How could you?" he cried, worse than Rose, "*How could you?* You just up and leave like that? Fake your death? And you'd planned it all out! You've had this planned for months, haven't you?" Kiara shrugged harshly. She was getting angry, too, "Well, yeah! I had to! You guys never let me out of your sight otherwise! What was I supposed to do? Say, 'Oh, hey, I have to go into this dangerous mission from which I might not come out alive, oh, and it also determines the fate of our kingdoms, so don't worry!' I'm not that stupid! And besides, this is what everyone wanted! Me dead! You brought me to Matthias to be killed! So what's the big deal?" James sighed angrily, "That was before I got to know you! You're my friend! I don't want you gone!"

Kiara groaned, "James, give it up! I'm not your friend! I can't be your friend! Just let it go, and get on with your life. You don't need me in it!" she gave him a look and continued descending the stairs.

"*Kiara to the Central Room! Kiara to the Central Room!*" came Anya's voice over the loudspeaker they'd had installed. Kiara ran into the Central Room, "What have we got?" she asked urgently. Tommy and Anya looked at her, "It's Rudy and his posse again. Nothing too serious." Anya said, rolling her eyes. Tommy shrugged, "They probably want their money and stuff back." Kiara sighed, "Yeah, fine, let them in." and then she turned to Nat and Reno, two of her new members, "Hey, you two, put the gang up in the balcony. Keep them up there, and keep them quiet, got it?" the two nodded, "Yes, Kiara!" and with the help of three others, they took the gang unwillingly up to the balcony.

Kiara went into the ballroom and waited for her guests. Within moments, they arrived. There was Roger Rudy, the leader of their so-called gang, with his groupies, Nadeen, Rocky, Jules, and Milo. They were all giving her looks.

Rudy went up to Kiara and shook her hand, "Kiara! Long time, no smoke! How ya been, darlin'?" Kiara laughed sarcastically, "Ah, you know me, always up to something!" and they both shared a good laugh at that. When they were done, Kiara motioned for Rudy and his associates to sit down. "Now, fellas," she asked, "what can I do for you? I doubt you're here for a simple reunion." Rudy looked at his buddies, "Well, Kiara, that's just it. It's past the due date for the money you owe us. We're startin' to think that you were just gonna leave us hangin'." Kiara rubbed her forehead. She'd sent the money a week ago, with Rich and Max. She hadn't seen them since, but Tommy had told her they'd delivered it. Kiara sighed, "Well, let's get this fixed." she gave Rudy a nod, whose pleasant demeanor returned. He nodded, "Great!"

"Tommy!" Kiara called into the next room. Tommy came into the ballroom, "Yeah?" she motioned for Tommy to come closer. "Tommy, didn't you say that Rich and Max had delivered our friend his money?" Kiara nodded towards Rudy, who bowed his head. Tommy looked at her, "Yeah, they said they delivered it." Kiara nodded, "Well, he claims he never received his payment. Why don't you locate the boys for me?" Tommy nodded, "Sure." and went over to the wall, where there was a small microphone and P.A. system.

"Messengers #478 and #586 to the Ballroom. Messengers #478 and #586 to the Ballroom." Tommy gave her a look, and after mindlessly chatting for a few minutes, two bodies popped into the room.

"You wanted to see us, Tommy?" one timid, pre-teen voice asked. Tommy sighed, "Not me. Kiara." and he waved towards her. Kiara motioned for the boys to come closer, "Rich, Max, Tommy tells me that you delivered the money we owed to Mr. Rudy over here. Is that true?" Rich and Max looked at each other nervously, and then at Rudy. "Well..." one of them started shakily, "We were going to, but—" then the other burst out, "The cops took the money! We barely got away with the rest of it! If it hadn't been for that James guy—" Kiara put up a hand quickly. "What? What 'James guy'? James who?" she could almost hear their heartbeats move faster and faster with each second. "Well?" Kiara shouted, "Who?" if she found out that James had helped them, she would kill him. No! She would hang him by his fingers and wait until his body weight broke his fingers and ripped his skin! Or she would slice her daggers throughout his body little by little, until he begged to be murdered. On second thought, she mused, she couldn't let his tainted blood stain her precious daggers.

Rich broke her out of her thoughts, "That cop guy! James Delarosa! You know, the guy who..." he didn't need to finish the sentence for Kiara to know what he was going to say. She sighed, "You're saying the cops took your money, or James took your money?" Max wrung his hand, "James took the money! He and those others, Captain Root and Holly Marx. The ones that you know so well. They stopped us, asking what we were doing. We tried to run away and attack them, but that James guy got really pissed, and took the money from us. Before we could do anything, they were gone." Kiara nodded, waved them away, and looked at Rudy.

"Well, Roger, I really am sorry about this mix-up. To make up for it, I'll pay you back right now, and you're invited to the convention tonight, my guest of honor. All expenses paid, and a free meal. How does that sound?" Bentley looked at the gang, who all gave subtle nods. He looked back at Kiara with a grin on his chubby face, "Perfect! I accept! No hard feelings, right, Kiara?" Kiara gave him a fake smile back, "Not a bit. Here, Tommy! Will you please show Mr. Rudy and his friends to the waiting room, and make sure to pay him in full. Also, mark down that his place is reserved for him at the table and in the front near the stage area." Tommy nodded, "Of course. Mr.

Rudy, would you please follow me?" Rudy and his gang stood up, and with a few handshakes and exchanged words, they left.

Kiara sighed, rubbed her forehead, and now, without so many distractions, heard the scuffling and muffled voices upstairs. "Jesus, guys, let 'em out, will you?" and without hesitation, seven bodies came tumbling down the stairs.

Captain Root started, "What the hell are you doing with him?" which was followed by Holly, "Are you insane? What is your deal?" which was followed by Gabriel, "You *owed* him? For *what?*" and then Felix, "I do think you're being a little rash about this, though you are his type to converse with," and Rose, "*Kiara*! Are you an *idiot?*" and finally James, who paused slightly before asking, "Kiara...what is wrong with you?"

Kiara gave a sarcastic chuckle, shrugged her shoulders, and started walking backwards towards the exit of the Ballroom. "James, don't you know? *Everything* is wrong with me." and with rolled eyes, she turned around and left the room, back to base, where Anya was conversing seriously with two Elites. "Anya!" Kiara called, and Anya looked at her, turned back, finished her instructions, and swiveled around in her chair to face me. "What can I do for you?" she asked dryly. Kiara sighed, "About the meeting tonight...what is the point of this, anyway?" Anya shrugged, "It's just a meeting of the most brilliant criminal minds in Lodos. We sit, we talk, we drink wine, people perform in the background, good food, a laugh, and business deals. Nothing new. Why?" Kiara grunted and glanced specifically back to where the gang was standing, "Them," she whispered, "they're not going anywhere anytime soon. What're we going to do about them while I'm entertaining my guests?" Anya sighed and leaned back in her chair. "Well," she said optimistically, "we could always stun them and bring them back to James' house, and by the time they woke up, it'd be tomorrow." Kiara nodded, but then quickly shot it down, "No, that won't work. We're out of stunners. New shipment won't be until the day after tomorrow." Anya grunted, "Damn. I was hoping for a chance to try out my new invention. Ah, well." and then she sighed, "Listen, Kiara, they're already here and know everything. Why don't you just let them come? On the conditions, of course. What can it hurt? If they sign the contract, they'll be ours anyway. And we can always stun them later if it doesn't work."

Kiara shrugged and sighed, "Fine. You bring up the contracts, the quills, the ink, anything you care to add in there. Now, I have to go make sure my dress fits. It's going to be a casino night tonight, and you know criminals and their casinos. It's like royalty at the ball." and with another smile, she left and went upstairs, to the balcony above the Ballroom, and opened the door behind the cedar chest that led to the attic which, no one knew, but was her personal study. Kiara sighed, not bothering to close the door, and went to the corner, where her friend Daelyn had helped her make a sleek black dress with red accents. She tied her red hair up into a thick, wavy ponytail, and even though she put it up, it still reached her shoulder blades.

"I never thought you were the dress type," Kiara heard from the doorway. She swung around, surprised to see James leaning against the doorpost. She sighed, "What do you want?" Kiara asked harshly, hoping to send him off. He just shrugged, "I need to talk to you. Now. This *cannot* wait." she sighed again, and after a minute of consideration, she saw that she wasn't going to win this argument. She waved him in, lit the several candles that provided the room's light, and turned to James. "What is it?"

James came two steps closer, "When did you plan on telling me you were alive?" Kiara rubbed the back of her neck, "I didn't," she said quietly, and watched him as he nodded, "So what did you plan to do the rest of your life? Steal, commit crimes, and live in secrecy?" Kiara thought it over, "That's the way you'd see it." James gave another nod and came a few steps closer, "Why did you do it?" Kiara sighed quietly, "I didn't want the attention, all you and the others ever wanted was for me to be arrested and 'brought to justice', and I was so sick of it. I was confused, angry, and I didn't want people like you in my life." James looked at her intensely, "People like me?" she shrugged and nodded, "Normal people, namely cops. The ones that think they know you but all they know is what you publicly put out there. They see the image. Not what it means." James took two steps closer, until he was less than an arm's length away. "Kiara...about your reply...you never answered me." Kiara nodded slightly. She knew.

"So answer it now," he told her huskily. He was now only an inch away. He leaned down to her, "because I meant every word, Kiara. I love you." She looked up in his eyes, beautiful and blue. She raised her mouth towards his, and their lips brushed for a second before, "Kiara?" James and Kiara both jumped and looked to the door, looking at Tommy, Anya, and the gang. Kiara snapped back into reality and pushed James away violently, becoming angry. "Go! Go *away*! What do you want here, anyway? I'm alive, okay? That's all you need to know! Now all of you just *go. Go,* and *never* come back!" when no one moved, she shouted even louder, "*Well?* What are you waiting for? *GO!*" and even then, they only moved slowly. Kiara groaned loudly and started to storm away.

"No." James grabbed her arm and swung her around, "No. You can't just run away whenever things come up that you don't know how to handle." At the mention of the words 'run away,' Kiara fumed. She grabbed her daggers from the corner and pointed one of them at James, "Get out of my way, or fight me."

James unsheathed his sword that was always at his side, "Fine." Kiara grunted and swung upward to hit him, but James blocked her move. With an agile turn she grazed his arm, drawing a flow of blood from his upper bicep. James swung out his sword, narrowly missing her face as she leaned backwards to dodge it. Putting her hands on the ground to hold herself up, she swung out one of her legs and successfully managed to bring James to the ground.

"Give *up*, Kiara!" James cried out as he swung out his sword, standing up. Kiara caught his sword with her daggers, "Never!" and pushed on his sword with all her might. James fell backwards and down to the ground again. Kiara sheathed her daggers and picked up his sword, holding it to his throat, "I will *never* give up!" she pressed the sword harder, drawing a minuscule amount of blood from his neck. All around them, time had stopped. The rest of them stood there, motionless, as the fight raged on. "Why? What could you possibly be fighting for all these years?" James choked. Kiara gave him a fierce look, "My way of life!" she breathed in and out heavily, "That's all I've *ever* fought for! My way of life! My freedom!" James looked at her, stunned, but before he could say a word, Kiara stood up slowly.

"Cancel the banquet. I can't do this anymore..." she said in a tired and shaky voice. She tossed his sword to the ground and backed up slowly, "I can't do this..." and with a slight push off, she began to run away from the scene. No one followed her, no one tried to stop her, no one did anything.

And that's the way she'd rather have it.

CHAPTER 8:

James stood up, watching as Kiara ran. Her flame-colored hair swished and cascaded as she bounced down the stairs, and soon, she was gone. Root came over to him urgently, "You okay, James?" James nodded, "Yeah, I'm fine." and looked down at his sword on the ground. He picked it up and sheathed it quickly.

Gabriel and Felix joined the group. "She's probably just going for a run." suggested Gabriel. Felix shook his head, "No way. She said she couldn't do this anymore. She meant the Messengers. She's running away. For real. Again." James groaned, "I can't lose her for another two years! That's happened twice already. I have to find her!" Root nodded, "We'll do everything we can to find her. But right now you need cleaned up. Come on. Let's go home."

—

"Okay, so if we were Kiara, where would we go?" is how Root started the meeting. Everyone sat and pondered for a few minutes. Rose nodded, "I'd do what I did the first time. Go to a new town and create a whole new identity. Become someone new." Gabriel nodded, "Of course. How did I not think of that?" Rose rolled her eyes, "Because I'm her friend and I know her. Now," she went to the map that hung on the wall of the conference room. "Here's the castle. And here's Kinkan. They're about a hundred miles away from each other. We should expect a place that's eighty to one hundred miles away to be her new area. She was headed west, but that means nothing. She'll probably turn directions every time she stops to rest for a minute or two. That's what Anya said they did the last time." She gasped, "Anya!"

—

Anya looked daggers at a sheepish James as they walked into the Messengers' common room, "Well, well, if it isn't lover boy and his gang of merry folk. What do you want now?" Root stepped forward, "We need to know where Kiara's going." Anya shook her head, "No way. I couldn't disclose that information even if I knew it." Tommy sighed, "Besides, she wants to be left alone. I say we respect her wishes, and she'll come back when she's cooled down and ready." James threw up his hands, "And when's that? Two years? Three? Never? We can't wait around for her to just show up! We have to look for her!" Root sighed. "Fine. It's not like no one would recognize her, so there's bound to be calls and alerts from the police. Tomorrow we'll call all of the precincts in expected area and see what leads we can get. Happy? Now go home. We all need some rest."

Rose sighed. James hadn't said anything at all the whole way home. She gave him a look. He shrugged, "You can make supper if you want. I'll be down in a while." Rose nodded, and reached out her hand to stop him from climbing the stairs. "Hey," she said, "do you need to talk? I'm always here. I'll listen." James smiled and patted her hand, "Thank you. Really. But right now I just need some rest." Rose nodded, "Okay. Come down when you're ready."

James walked slowly up the stairs to his room. His room wasn't colorful or full of trinkets; it consisted of a bed with black sheets and blankets, black dressers and a desk, off-white walls and curtains, and a few personal items. This had been his room ever since he was little. Through the years, he'd added more personal items here and there. A shield, an extra sword, a few books, pictures, and the like. He sighed and sat down on his bed. He pulled out his cell phone (given to him by the department for work) and flipped it open. How he wished Kiara had a phone. He'd give anything to hear her speak to him again, to hear her rare laugh. He didn't understand. What was so wrong with a little help? Everyone needs help sometimes. And why couldn't she just work with them? They wanted to help the Messengers. She didn't realize that what she was doing was wrong, and that she needed to follow the law. If she did that, they'd leave her alone. He flopped down onto his back and groaned. What did he do now? He had to find her, but did she even want to be found? There's always a reason people run away, and maybe he just needed to give her space.

But no, he couldn't do that! Absolutely not! She needed someone to take care of her, someone to help her. She couldn't do everything by herself! And in turn, he needed her. He'd never felt this way before. He loved her. There was something about her, her captivating smile, her fierce and independent spirit, the way she faced each day with such bravery. She was special. She always had been.

Special. That's what she hated about herself. Being different, being odd, being something that no one else could understand. She'd always been persecuted for it. And there was nothing anyone could do about it. Nothing she could do about it. She couldn't control it, and that's what she hated. All she'd ever wanted was a normal life. But she would never get it. She would never have that. So she rebelled.

"James?" Rose stood in the doorway tentatively. James sighed, "Come on in." Rose sat down next to him. "What's really bugging you? Come on. Speak." James groaned, "It's just...I don't understand. Why does she think running is the only solution? It doesn't make sense!" Rose shrugged, "Because no one's ever showed her another solution. Not to her satisfaction, anyway. You want her back, you surpass her expectations." James sat up and gave her a look, "What do you mean?" Rose raised her eyebrows, "She thinks that everyone's going to come looking for her and try to find her through police means. She thinks that no one wants her as *her*. As a person. She expects to see wanted posters all over and to have to hide. Don't do anything like that. Find out what town she's in, and go to find her yourself. She doesn't think you want to find her because you love her. She thinks you want to find her because it's your job." James nodded, "Then I'll find her. On my own. I'll find her and bring her back. Because I want to." Rose looked at him with a smile, "There he is! I wondered where you'd gone."

Kiara stopped and put her hands on her knees. She'd been running for hours, mile after mile. She hadn't run into any roads or towns, so she assumed that she was in a remote area of forest. She looked up and took note of her surroundings. There were trees, tall, thick, and covered in moss, a few ground-level plants, but nothing more. No paths, no roads, no nothing. She sighed and put her head in her hands.

"Frustrated, are we?" Kiara whipped around, startled, and saw James with his back to her, blonde hair, black T-shirt and all. She narrowed her eyes, "James? What are you doing here? What do you want?" James chuckled and turned around. "I'm not James." and Kiara immediately spotted the differences. This man was slightly more muscular, with a sharper, more defined face. His eyes were a deep blue instead of a sky-blue color. His hair was sandy brown, no trace of blonde whatsoever. She took a step back, "Who are you?" the man stuck out his hand, "Calvin. I assume you're Kiara?" Kiara nodded without returning the greeting. He looked at his hand, shrugged, and let it fall to his side. "What's the matter?" he asked. Kiara brushed him off, "Nothing. Leave me alone." Calvin came behind her and put his hand on her shoulder, "Hey, I'm sorry. I didn't mean to trick you or anything. I know who I must look like. You just looked really frustrated. I thought I could help." Kiara sighed. He sounded sincere, and maybe he was. She shrugged, "I've been looking for a path. Any path. To anywhere. I've been traveling a long time." Calvin smiled, "Well, you're in luck. I know these woods like the back of my hand. See that really big tree with the knotted branch?" Kiara nodded, "Go past that, turn right, and you'll see some birch trees. Go through about five of those, and off to your left, there'll be a path that leads you to a small village." She looked at Calvin, "You're serious?" Calvin looked seriously at her, "Yeah. No joke." Kiara nodded, "Alright then. Well, thank you." she turned around to leave, and thought she'd turn back to ask what village, but Calvin was gone.

That's strange, she thought, *he was just here a second ago.* Shrugging, she followed his instructions carefully. There *was* a path. He'd been right. It wound around a tree, but she couldn't see where it led. He'd said it led to a village, so she inwardly sighed, and carried on.

The path went on forever, and soon, Kiara thought that she might be more lost than she previously had been. She groaned inwardly. How could she be so stupid? You never follow paths that you don't know, especially when given by strangers! And now it was almost sundown. In another two hours, the world would succumb to darkness, and then what? She couldn't travel; she'd have to camp. Camping in an unfamiliar place was always a terrible idea. She didn't know what kind of animals or people were around, whether these were free range hunting grounds or abandoned woods. She kept on with the path, hoping that it would lead her somewhere.

The forest on its own was creepy. Spider webs were everywhere, the trees were knotted and twisted, the wind made eerie sounds through the hollows of fallen logs. She wanted out of here. She wanted this path to lead her to a village, like Calvin had said!

Just before sundown, the path came to rest at a very small village with wooden cottages and thatched rooftops. There didn't seem to be any modern technology. She imagined this to be one of the old villages her father had told her about as a child. These villages refused to advance with the rest of the world. They liked their simple ways, and they intended to stay that way.

She went up to a woman in a rocking chair, next to a well. The woman was knitting silver wool, and was humming to herself. Kiara gathered up her courage, hoping this woman wouldn't recognize her. "Um...ma'am?" she asked quietly, and was surprised at the raspy quality of her voice. The woman looked up and smiled, "Yes, dearie. What can I do for you?" Kiara looked to the well, "Could I have a drink of water please?" The woman beamed, "Of course. Here." she pulled up the bucket from the well and dunked a wooden cup into the clear water. Kiara drank that down and stuck the cup out for more. The woman chuckled and gave her cup after cup of crisp, cool water, until her thirst was no more.

"Thank you." she said with a small smile. She was very grateful to this kind woman. She nodded to her, and turned around. The old woman stood up, "Where are you going?" Kiara turned around and sighed, "I don't know." she said truthfully. The woman nodded, "Come inside, dearie. You look in need of a hot meal and a good rest." Kiara smiled softly, "Thank you, ma'am." the woman shook her head, "Call me Mabel."

Mabel led Kiara into her home, which was very humble. Most everything was wooden or cloth, and there consisted of a small kitchen area, a table and two chairs, and two doors that led to two bedrooms. Mabel went over to her kitchen, where a pot was sitting over a fire. She took a large, wooden spoon, and stirred it a little, tasting the product. She nodded with a blissful smile, and turned to Kiara, "Stew's just about ready. Why don't you have a bath before supper? You look like you could use one, dearie." Kiara shrugged, and looked down at herself. Dirty as the forest floor, her legs were covered in soot, her clothes grass-stained and torn. God only knew how her hair looked. She let Mabel lead her into a separate door she hadn't seen. There was a small mirror, a wooden bathtub, and a washbowl for a sink.

Mabel filled the bathtub with hot water and lavender salts, and handed her a white, cotton dress. "Here you go. Used to be my daughter's. She wore that all the time. I apologize if it's too big. You're a small one for your age." Kiara shook her head, "No. Thank you. No one's been this kind to me in a very long time." The old woman's eyes lit up, "Well, we're starting anew, aren't we?" and she left.

Kiara shed her clothes and set them aside. She stepped into the perfectly warm tub, and let herself sit down and sigh. Her hair fanned out around her, and she sank into the water, letting herself be immersed in its tranquility. She took a sponge from the shelf beside her and scrubbed her incredibly dirty skin until it was gleaming white. With some soap from the same shelf, she washed her hair over and over until its red brilliance and softness had returned. By the time she stepped out of the bath, the water was a dirty, murky color. Satisfied, Kiara took the white cotton dress and slipped it on. It was the perfect size, and was thin enough to be cool, but thick enough to be warm and heavy. She smiled at her reflection. She could barely see the scar that ran across her face. She looked almost...well, almost normal.

"Oh, there you are! Well, don't you look a sight!" Mabel exclaimed when Kiara joined her in the kitchen area. Kiara smiled a little and shrugged, "Thank you." she said again. The woman nodded, and an almost sorrowful look came onto her face. Kiara frowned, "What's the matter? Did I do something?" the woman shook herself out of her stupor, "Hmm? Oh, no! No, not at all. It's just, well, you look so much like my daughter that I...oh, memories." Kiara nodded, "Who was your daughter?" Mabel smiled, "Her name was Kassi. She lived in a little-known land off the South coast of Lodos. Came back with twins, of all things! A boy and a girl. She died not a year later. Never saw the children again. I suppose they're living with their father. A big important one up North. Oh, the stew!" she grabbed two bowls and a ladle and spooned the thick, rich soup into each of them. She gave a bowl and a wooden spoon to Kiara. "There you are. Best stew this side of the forest, I guarantee it!"

Kiara sat down across from Mabel, and tasted the stew. It was creamy and warm, rich with the earthy flavors of broth, carrots, and potatoes. There were wild onions mixed in, adding a tangy flavor to the earthiness. This was the best food she'd had in years, and she asked for another bowl. And another. The old woman laughed, "Well, now. It's good to see such an appetite from such a thin girl. Now, tell me, child, what brings you up here to these parts? You don't look like you're from around here." Kiara put her spoon down. "I don't know, to be honest. It's a little complicated." the old woman nodded, "Well, let's hear it then. The whole and honest truth. No sense in lying to an old widow like me."

Kiara groaned, "I was born special. Too special. Almost everyone hates me because I'm the Dark Faelis. I ran away with my little sister when I was eight, and everything got screwed up. We got caught and ran away countless times, again and again. We joined the Messengers, which was a corrupted organization of criminal children to get money. I ran away from that, and came back later to take over. I created a new home for runaways and kids like them. Street kids. But I was never happy. I was so corrupted with all this power that came from fear. I realized when I was almost used for that power to kill my brother that I needed to stop, so when I returned home, I locked myself in my room and spoke to no one. They thought I was dead. Then I fought my friend James. I know he loves me, he's said it more than once. But I just...I couldn't! I couldn't be with him! He was my enemy, and we're complete opposites! And I realized that I couldn't do it anymore. So I ran away again. And here I am." Mabel nodded, "Seems like you've done an awful lot of running." Kiara looked at her folded hands in her lap and spoke quietly, "Yeah. I have." the old woman took her hand, "So where do you want to go now?" Kiara shrugged, "I have no idea. I don't know what to do."

"Well, it's quite simple. Just be the princess." Kiara looked at the woman, shocked. "What?" she asked incredulously. The woman laughed, "Don't think I don't know the lost princess of Lodos when I see her! Now come on! You're the princess! You're supposed to be running this place!" Kiara shook her head, "I gave up that right a long time ago. Besides, no one wants me as their princess." Mabel stood up, "That's because you've never given them a reason to want you. You were young and they were fearful and judgmental, no one could help it. Had you stayed, maybe things would be different. But they aren't. They'll hold to their views until you prove them wrong. It is your right and responsibility as princess and Faelis to lead and rule your people. It's what you were born to do." Kiara looked at her, "Do you really think that?" Mabel nodded, "Of course! Now come on! Do you want to be angry and lost for the rest of your life? It's time you find yourself."

"Find myself? What do you mean? Where would I even start?" Mabel gave her a look, "You think I believe for one moment that you are a true criminal or an evil person? After the good manners and warm heart you've proved to have in the hours I've known you? That's not you. Well, maybe part of it is. The fighting part will always be something that you can't resist, because that's who you are. But you're not a thief. You're no killer. You're a lost, scared young girl that's been the target of countless arrows. You're a princess, brave and kind and strong. That's who you are, not the mask you put on when you wake up in the morning." Kiara shrugged, "Yeah, well, that's not what others would say." Mabel leaned in closer to her, "That's because they don't know the real you. You've never revealed yourself. You're a talented actress, and you do well at keeping your mask in place. If they knew who you really were, they'd say the same things I did."

Did she really believe that? Kiara had never been talked to like that, with an unconditionally loving tone, not since Ana died. She sighed, "So where do I start?" Mabel took a good, long moment of thought before answering, "Get to know your people. You know how to be a princess, but that's not all a ruler needs to know. A good ruler knows their people. Interacts with them. Go live with them. Help them. Make a difference. That's the foundation of a great leader." Kiara snorted and laughed, "Interact with them? Look at me! *Everybody* knows me! I'll be phoned in as soon as I'm seen, and then my friends will come and gather me. It'll never work." Mabel closed her eyes, and then jumped suddenly, "Oh!" she quickly went to a separate room, one that Kiara had missed, and stepped into the magical space. There were potions, wands, cauldrons, a cloak, and books of all sorts. Kiara watched as Mabel went to her potions shelf, rummaged around, and pulled out a glowing purple vial. Kiara finally found her voice, "You're a witch!" Mabel shrugged, "And you're a Faelis. If we resign ourselves to labels, soon we'll all be kitchen utensils. Now come here, and sit down." Kiara did as she was told, and sat in a chair. Mabel grabbed a comb and cup of water, and dipped the comb into the cup, running it through her hair until her hair was thoroughly damp. She took the vial and poured it into the water, continuing the process. Kiara felt a tingling sensation on her scalp, and it intensified with each stroke of the comb. When the woman was done, she grabbed a new cup of water, and slowly poured it down her hair, kneading it until she was satisfied. With a snap of her fingers, Kiara's hair was dry.

"There! Now no one will recognize you!" Kiara gave the woman a look, "What do you mean?" Mabel pulled out a hand mirror and gave it to Kiara. She gasped, "My hair! It's brown!" Mabel nodded, "But it's only temporary. It'll last you a few weeks. Got it? And every day, the color will

fade. At the end of three weeks, it will be back to normal."
Kiara looked at her, "I have three weeks to win over my
people, go home, convince my guardians that I'm okay and
ready to rule, and present myself to all of my people, and
win all of *them* over?" Mabel nodded, "I wouldn't give you
anything you couldn't do. You can do this. I know you can.
You have my daughter's fire in you." Kiara looked down at
her lap, "I can't tell you how much this means to me. To
have someone believe in me." she looked up with tears in
her eyes, "Thank you." she whispered. Mabel wiped away
her tears with a smile, "Come now. Let's get you to bed."
She took Kiara to the room next to the kitchen, and smiled
at her, "Get some rest now. We'll see you off in the
morning."

That night, Kiara didn't dream. She didn't stir in her
sleep. She didn't cry. She simply rested, and was at peace
for the first time since she could remember.

—

"You're going to be okay, right?" Root looked up at
James, mounted on Rhian. Rose laughed, "I think he'll be
fine. You've been asking him that for hours!" Root blushed
slightly, "Well, I...I can't risk having my finest employee
gone for good!" he put out as an excuse. Rose sighed and
looked up at James, "You good?" James nodded, "Yeah. I
think I'm good. I'll just follow the trail and see if anyone's
seen her. I'll be back. I promise. And I'll write." Rose took
his hand, "Good luck, James. Bring her home safe for us,
okay?" James nodded and smiled a little, "I will. Goodbye,

Rose." With a few more goodbyes and waving, James headed off into the dense forest, looking back just once.

"You have *got* to be kidding me!" this was the fifth dead end that Rhian and the trail had led him to. He'd been led to a cave, which he thoroughly inspected, with no sign of human life. Then he'd been taken to a rock wall, impossible to scale, and then a large river, which he suspected she might have taken, and then decided not, because Kiara was not so stupid as to jump into a freezing river with deadly fish larger than herself.

"What's wrong, bro?" James turned to the side, looking at a man similar in appearance to himself. He narrowed his eyes, "What do you want?" the man shrugged with an amused face, "Still looking for your girl, huh? You're doing an awful lot of chasing, James. Not enough romancing, I think. That's your problem." James rolled his eyes, "As if you'd know anything about her. Screw off, Calvin." Calvin almost laughed, "Me? Know about her? No, you're right, not much. But I know a hell of a lot more than you do." James furrowed his brows in angry confusion, "What do you mean?" Calvin shrugged, "She and I. We're the same. Unlike you, I understand her. And that's all she really wants. I can give her that. You can't." James unsheathed his sword, "You don't know that!" Calvin retreated, "Maybe not on my own, but hey, it came from her mouth. Not mine." and with a last wink, he retreated into the woods.

James was utterly confused. He'd spoken to her?
When? Where? She'd told him this? Why? Was he serious,
or was he just playing him? What did he mean 'we're the
same'? He shook his head. Rhian would follow Calvin's
path. With any hope, it would lead him to Kiara.

—

Kiara woke up from her surprisingly undisturbed sleep.
She smiled and hugged herself. She felt well-rested and
awake; stress free. Slowly, she got up, made her bed,
shrugged off the nightgown she'd been given, and put on
the white cotton dress from the day before. She yanked a
strip of leather off of her wrist, and tied her hair in a knot.
Much to her dismay, a few curled strands were hanging
loose, but she ignored it.

"Oh, dear, you're up! Good! Breakfast is ready!" Kiara
followed Mabel out to the kitchen, where there was a
breakfast feast of apples, fresh-squeezed orange juice, bread,
cheese, oats and milk, honey, cream, jam, and tea. She
couldn't help but to sit down and grab one helping of
everything. Mabel laughed whole-heartedly, "I haven't seen
anyone eat so much since my daughter was here!" Kiara
laughed, but she was so hungry. She ate quickly, and stood
as the sun rose past the sunrise. Mabel looked at her, "Well,
you'd best be on your way." Kiara nodded, and accepted
the cloth bag from Mabel.

"Now, in there's a lunch pack: two slices of bread,
three pieces of cheese, an apple, some cooked meat, and a
skin with milk in it. Be careful not to eat it too late, or it'll

spoil. There's another dress, a blue one I found in the attic. I didn't see you wearing shoes when you came. Did you want some? I have an extra pair." Kiara shook her head, "No thank you. I'm not really a fan of shoes." the woman shrugged, "Suit yourself. There's your knives and belt in there, unfortunately, your clothes were unsalvageable. There's also a pouch of Youans. About ten, I think. It's the currency in this part of the country. Thought you could use it for backup. Now, there's a village called Jinora to the South. If you go into the forest from here, you'll find a small road, and that'll lead you straight to it in about an hours' time. It's a smaller town, but growing. You can stay there." Kiara looked at her, trying not to cry, "Thank you. Thank you so much. How can I repay you?" the woman shook her head, "Don't worry about it. Just promise me you'll mend what's been done wrong." embracing the woman in a tight squeeze, she whispered her promise, "I will." and broke away from her hug. With a smile and another, "Thank you," she went on her way.

The sun was high in the sky, it was probably around noon. Kiara hadn't broken down to eat her lunch yet, but then, she wasn't really hungry. She was nervous. How could she just do this? Everyone knew her. She had a reputation, one that she used to think she had to uphold. It was hard to tear away from her past this suddenly, but she knew it had to be done. She couldn't stay like this. It wouldn't get her anywhere. She had to change her fate. But how? Everyone would recognize her. She'd be found out in no time. And then what? Would she go back? Would she be dragged back? Would she just run away again? What would happen then? The thought of the unknown just...disturbed her.

Off in the distance, she could hear the rumble of a motorcycle and people talking. That had to be the town. Kiara took a deep breath. She could do this. She could do this! She had to. It was only another half mile before she reached the town.

There were people everywhere. Some of them were dressed like her: simple and plain. Others wore jeans and T-shirts, people standing behind fruit and vegetable and fish and meat stands wore leather aprons, putting products into scales and taking coins from the customers. Nobody really paid attention to her. For the first time in her life since becoming Kiara Santiago, she seemed invisible.

"So, what's it like, being normal?" Kiara jumped at the voice of the man next to her. She looked up, "Calvin?" Calvin smiled his lopsided smile, "Hey, what's up?" Kiara glared at him, "What are you doing here, and how did you recognize me?" he put up his hands, "Whoa. After the help I gave you, I thought you'd be glad to see me. And it's not really that hard since I've seen you before." Kiara sighed, "I'm sorry. I've just been freaking out for a few hours." Calvin looked around, "Come with me. We can talk somewhere else." he grabbed her hand and led her to a small, grassy park. He sat down underneath a tree and patted the grass beside him. "Come on. Tell me everything."

"Later," Kiara said. Calvin shrugged, "Well, I do have to admit, you look ten times more beautiful after a bath than you did in the woods the other day. And your hair...it's still so beautiful. Though I do miss the red curls." Kiara laughed, "Yeah, me too. But if it gets me somewhere, it's worth it. Besides, it'll only last a few weeks. Then it'll turn back to red. And everyone will know who I am." Calvin nodded, "Then let's get started. Tomorrow. It's almost sundown, anyway. Where are you staying? I'll walk you there." Kiara looked at the ground, "I...um...well..." Calvin sighed, "You don't have a place to stay, do you? Of course not. Well, come on. Let's get you to an inn. On me."

James knew that Rhian was beat. He'd finally found a path to a village, and when he saw the well of water in front of a shop, he couldn't resist but to knock on the door. When an old woman answered, he felt bad for knocking at this time of evening. "Yes, dear? What can I help you with?" James was relieved that she wasn't upset with him for his rudeness. "My horse is really thirsty. Could you give us some water, please?" the woman smiled, "You're the second person this week coming to ask for water." James looked at her, "Oh?" the woman nodded and let the bucket down into the well, "Yes. A young girl came just yesterday, poor thing. Tired to the bone, dirty as a rat. More lost than a blind man in a maze with no end." James looked at her with curiosity, "Really? She sounds like someone I know. What did she look like?" the woman raised the bucket and set it on the ground in front of Rhian, "Brown hair. Green eyes. Pale as the moon." James slumped slightly, discouraged, "Oh. I see."

"You should go look for her." James looked up at her, "What?" the woman slapped his shoulder, "Go look for her! You look in need of a quest. She can help you with whatever your troubles are right now." James snorted, "There's only one girl who can do that." the woman shrugged, "And how do you know she's not it? There's only one person for everybody, but you'll never know if you never try." James shook his head, "No, I'm looking for someone else." the woman gave him a glare, "If you don't go look for her, I'll make you do it. Don't underestimate me. Now, I've lived a score of years longer than you. I know leagues more than you do. So when I say to do something, it is for the good of everything, including yourself, and you will do it! Do I make myself clear?" James was shocked from the outburst from the woman. He nodded timidly, and she smiled. "Good. Do you know the village of Jinora?" he nodded, "My friend lives there." she beamed, "Good. Go to that village. Find her." James nodded, "I will, then." and with a shy, "Thank you," he got on his horse, and headed for Jinora.

"Remind me again why you got a room for two?" Kiara looked suspiciously at Calvin. He shrugged innocently, "I don't feel like going home. Besides, you don't know this place. You need someone to guide you around." he glanced over to her and laughed at the look she was giving him, "What, you think I want to get laid or something tonight? Nah, dude, come on. I'm being serious. But hey, if you're into it, I mean, I can't deny a lady, right?" Kiara rolled her eyes and laughed, "Thanks for the offer, but I think I'll pass." Calvin smiled, "Whatever you say. What's in the bag?" Kiara looked at it and shrugged, "Some money, food, another dress, my daggers and belt." he looked at her with a sly eye, "I'd like to see you in another dress." Kiara threw a pillow at him, "Seriously!" he laughed, "Okay, okay, but really. Did you say food?" Kiara snorted, "Yes, you pig. Here." she reached into the bag and tossed the pack and skin at him. He looked at her with an offended glance, "Pig? You've known me for one day! And you haven't even seen me eat!" Kiara sat down on his bed next to him. "Very well. You're not a pig. Yet." he took out the bread and cheese, "Thank you. What, no meat?" Kiara shrugged, "Left it in the forest for an animal. Didn't think I'd be sharing my lunch with someone." he looked at her, appalled, "What are you? A vegetarian?" Kiara nodded, "I don't like meat. It tastes gross."

"Not even bacon?!" Kiara shook her head fervently and smiled, "No! What is it with people and bacon?" Calvin stood up, "Bacon is the food of the gods. And I can't share a sitting place with an herbivore." and he sat cross-legged on the ground. Kiara shook her head, "Whatever." and they sat there in silence for a few moments. After a while, Calvin turned towards her, soft-faced and serious, "What are you doing out here, anyway? Shouldn't you be in Kinkan, fighting the local police force for some rebel cause?" Kiara flopped down on the bed and shrugged, "Maybe. I don't know. I just...I got so sick of it. The repetition. The same routine every single day. You know, with the Messengers. It was boring, above all. And it just didn't feel right. I felt...out of place. So after the last big fight with James and the guys, I decided I couldn't keep doing that anymore. So I went on my own. I found this old lady in that town you pointed me to. She told me I reminded her of Kassi, her daughter, who'd lived in a remote island up north and came back with twins who had no father. They live with some important guy up North, she said. Anyway, I told her about my life. It was something I'd never done before. And she said to come here."

Calvin flipped onto his stomach, "Why?" Kiara twirled her hair, "Because in order to be the princess I'm supposed to be, I need to interact with my people. I'm not going to be one of those princesses whose sole goal in life is to find true love and live happily ever after. I want to change things. I want to change the way things are. I want everyone to have the life they deserve. And since I already took my crash course in Princess 101, I can focus on some fieldwork. See what's *really* going on." Calvin smiled, "You're amazing, you know that?" Kiara snorted, "Whatever." and looked at Calvin, whose face had creased in thought, "What?" Calvin looked at her, "Do you know who that lady was?" Kiara nodded, "Her name was Mabel. Why?" Calvin's eyes widened, "Mabel? And her daughter's name is Kassi? With that story you told me?" Kiara nodded, and Calvin blanched, "Kiara, don't you know who that was?" Kiara shook her head, "No."

Calvin stood up and pulled her off of the bed, "That was the former queen of Lodos. Queen Mabel. She left the throne to her good friend, Garren, after her daughter ran away. When her daughter came back with twins, and died, the twins were handed over to the king and queen as the rightful heirs to the throne." Kiara's breathing quickened. She had a bad feeling, "So?" Calvin whispered to her, "That was your grandmother."

Kiara sat down quickly on the bed, "What do you mean?" Calvin paced the room, "Everyone knows that you and Rowan—yes, I know about Rowan—aren't the children of Queen Ana and King Garren. You're twins. And Mabel—she said you reminded her of her daughter. Of course. It all fits together." Kiara raised an eyebrow, "That in no way proves that she's my grandmother." Calvin pointed at her, "Yes it does. None of the other children are adopted. None of them. You and Rowan are the only ones, and you know it. Besides, if these two children had died, you can bet your ass it would be all over the news. That lady, Kassi, was your mother." Kiara shook her head, "You can't prove that! My mother died when I was a baby!" Calvin raised an eyebrow, "Maybe she died when you were a toddler."

Kiara punched him in the arm, "Whatever! Shut up! Just leave me alone! I'm going to bed!" and with an angry grunt, she turned off the light, and went to sleep.

"Kiara?" it was the middle of the night, and Calvin hadn't fallen asleep once. In fact, he wasn't even tired. He was upset—upset with her, mostly. She had no right to be mad at him! He knew it was the truth! He'd known who she was, what she was. He'd known who her mother was. He knew everything about her. Granted, he didn't know the old lady was her grandmother, but other than that, he knew what he was talking about! She had no right to tell him he was wrong when she knew he was right!

He turned on the lamp, grateful that the light bulb was dim, and softened when he saw her face. She looked so sad. Here was this girl who'd been tortured her whole life, who had to fight with all she had, every day, just to keep doing what she knew, and he was persecuting her in his mind. Just like everyone else. He wanted to slap himself. What was he thinking? She was just in denial. He'd been there before. All of the previous anger had been washed away by her face. He sighed, stood up, and sat down next to her still body, "Kiara?" he whispered, and shook her a little. Kiara's eyes fluttered open and she looked up at him, "What?"

"I'm sorry. About before. I had no right to say those things." Kiara sat up and sighed, "It's fine. I knew you were right. I just…I've been told nothing about my real family. All I have is a few words and an image in my mind of what it would have been like. I always thought that I would be the one to find out who they were. Or Rowan. But when you said all that, I got upset because it wasn't me who discovered it." Calvin shrugged, "Hey, I get it. I'd feel the same way. So...do you forgive me?" Kiara smiled a little, "Yeah. I forgive you." and with a yawn, she laid back down, "Goodnight, Calvin." Calvin stood up and went back to his bed, "Goodnight."

After she was sure he was asleep, Kiara got up and out of bed. She wasn't tired; she couldn't sleep. She picked up her bag and headed for the window. She needed some fresh air.

She gasped as she tripped over her own feet, and the bag went skidding across the floor. She quickly looked to see if Calvin had awoken, but he was still fast asleep. She sighed in relief, and went to pick up her bag. Something on the floor glinted in the light. She picked it up. It was the locket. James' locket. How had that gotten in there? She'd taken it off and left it at Mabel's house specifically so she could forget about James. Of course Mabel had put it in there. Mabel always knew what to do.

What was she supposed to do now? She had to forget about James. She didn't love him. She couldn't love him. But she missed him, more than she'd let herself in the last few years. She was so torn. She couldn't love him, right? She was a street kid.

Not anymore, though. She was going to be the princess now. And he was the prince of Alacrast. It was almost like…no. Kiara would *not* let herself think that. They were not meant for each other. What a stupid line. What was she thinking?

Kiara sighed quietly and left her bag. She didn't need it. She just needed to get out of the room. Silently, she climbed onto the window ledge, and jumped.

James had been in this town for hours, and he'd seen no sign of the brown-haired girl. He'd seen plenty of girls with brown hair, but none that fit the woman's description. What was the big deal, anyway? What was so special about her? He should be looking for Kiara, not wasting his time in this stupid town!

It was near two a.m., and at this time of night, Jinora might as well have been a ghost town. There was no way that Kiara was here. This town was small, compact. He hadn't seen any sign of skyscrapers or large fountains in front of buildings or clubs. It just wasn't her scene. There was no way she'd stay here.

Ugh! He was so angry with himself. He never should have listened to that crazy old woman! What an idiot he was. Oh, yeah. Go ahead. Just take orders from any old crazy lady. Because that's a completely sane thing to do! Ugh!

Wait, what was that? He saw something moving near a small pool of water in one of the cobblestone streets. He got off his horse, tied him to a tree, and walked silently towards the figure. As he got closer, he could see that it was a girl. She was kneeling next to the pool, looking at something in her hands by the light of the moon. With a gasp, she flung the thing and fell backwards. "No!" she cried quietly. James hurried over to her and picked up the object, a small, golden locket. He looked at her face, and gasped. Kiara! He could see her green eyes, and the scar across her face!

"Kiara?" he asked, a little too loudly. The girl looked at him with horror in her face, and then slowly shook her head, "Who? I'm not Kiara." he looked at her more closely, "Yes, you are! Kiara! What are you doing here? I've been looking for you for two days!" the girl stood up and shook her head, "I'm not Kiara. I don't know what you're talking about." he stepped closer to the girl, and realized his mistake. Her hair was brown. A deep, rich chestnut brown. He stuck out the locket, "Oh, I'm sorry. I mistook you for a friend. I'm very, very sorry." the girl took the locket tentatively and shrugged, "It's okay." he nodded, "Alright, then. I'll be on my way. Sorry, again." and with a sigh, he started off towards his horse. *Stupid!* He thought to himself, *what's wrong with you? Stupid!* And with an angry demeanor, he climbed upon his horse, and looked at the girl, who was running off, and realized his mistake.

It was the girl he'd been sent to find.

—

Kiara flopped down on her bed and let out the breath she'd been holding. She couldn't believe that he was here. And he'd recognized her! Of course he'd recognized her. But then...had he believed her? When she said she wasn't Kiara? She didn't know. She couldn't be sure. But she had to trust that he had. If he hadn't believed her, he'd have said something, right? He would have taken her right back to Kinkan for sure. She nodded in assurance. He would have. She was safe.

Kiara rolled onto her side and sighed. She had to let go of him. She had a mission to complete. A legacy to fulfill. That was her top priority and nothing else. She had to ignore him and just carry on with her task. She would do it. She could do it. She could change. She would take back her kingdom. She would do it for the kids, to create a new system. She would make their world better, and she could do it with the influence and power of the status she had to achieve.

And she would start tomorrow.

Calvin opened his eyes and yawned. He'd had a pretty good night of sleep. No dreams, no waking up, no tossing and turning. Yep, he felt good! He sat up and looked around.

Where was Kiara?

Calvin raced up out of bed and scoured the room. She wasn't here. He pulled on a shirt and jeans, and without bothering to do anything else, he raced out of the inn and into the streets. "Have you seen a girl with a white dress and brown hair?" he asked everyone he met on the street. They all said no. Calvin groaned. He knew this would happen! He knew she would run away! Of course she would! Of course!

"Mister?" Calvin looked up, and saw a little girl, poor, from the looks of it, with a piece of bread stuck out to him. Calvin looked at her, "Yes?" the girl urged the bread piece towards him, "Here. For you." he took the bread and scrutinized her. She was dirty, with a ragged dress and matted hair, with no shoes. "Why are you giving this to me? Where did you get this?" the little girl pointed to a crowd of children and poor people in the distance, "There's a lady giving bread and milk for us to give to others. Here you go!" and with a small smile, she ran away.

A lady giving bread and milk and telling stories? Who was she? Jesus? Calvin shook his head and walked with fervor towards the crowd. He pushed through them, and was about to confront this lady, when he stopped. Kiara looked up at him, "What's up?" Calvin gave her a look, "What are you doing?" Kiara looked around, "These people need help. They need food. They need hope." Calvin shrugged, "So? They can get it themselves. Come on." he grabbed her and dragged her away, "Calvin!" she cried out, and tried to break herself from his grasp, "Let go of me!" he shook his head and stopped near a park, remote from the village people. "What the hell are you doing?" Kiara looked around and scoffed, "Helping. Like I said." Calvin raised his arms, "Why? You've got your own problems. They have theirs." Kiara fumed, "I know what they've been through! I've felt their pain, their hunger! I can't just let them fend for themselves! They have no idea how!" Calvin shrugged, "Neither did you. You learned!" Kiara shook her head,

"Calvin, I learned when I was five. I was taught by a pack of werewolves. I had an advantage. They don't."

Calvin shook his head and turned around, "Whatever. I just don't get why you feel so...helpful...all of a sudden. I thought you were a fighter. Some activist with a tough side. But this...this isn't you. You're the enemy, not the savior, remember?" Kiara clenched her fists in rage, "You don't know me! You don't know anything about me! I am a fighter! I fight for those who can't fight for themselves! I will always fight for them! But they need help, and whatever they need, I'm going to give them, because I'd want them to do the same for me. And I may not be their savior, but I am sure as hell going to do my best to be the person that they can turn to. I'm not the enemy anymore." and with an angry sigh, she stalked away. Calvin stood there, staring at her. *What is she doing?* He thought. *She isn't turning Light, is she? No, that's her brother. But...the curse...it's wearing off.*

I have to tell Nicodemus.

For Kiara, this wasn't easy. It was instinct for her to walk around carefully, scouring the streets for police, but it was another thing to pass right by them and have them smile at her. It made her feel odd each time. She supposed she'd just have to get used to it. By now she didn't care. That fight with Calvin had wired her up. What did he think she was doing? Kiara had told him from the beginning about what

Mabel told her to do! Why was he acting so surprised? What was his problem?

"Kiara? Kiara!" Kiara froze. Who was calling her name? She turned around, and saw a man with black hair and a joyful face jogging towards her. When he came closer, he slowed down, "Whoa, girl, you changed your hair." Kiara couldn't believe who was standing in front of her. It was Christian, an old Messenger member. He'd grown too old to be a part of it, so he'd moved out. Kiara smiled with relief and ran to hug him, "Christian!" she cried, and he twirled her around as she clung to his neck. "Christian, what are you doing here?" Christian laughed, "I should ask you the same question. I'm doing some work here with my mom. I have an apartment. What about you?" Kiara sighed, "It's a long story." Christian shrugged, "Well, come on. We can go to my apartment and talk about it. You look hungry. Even if you aren't, I'm hungry." Gratefully, Kiara nodded, and went along with him.

CHAPTER 9:

"*That's* what you're doing here? Becoming a princess? A little cliché, don't you think?" Kiara sighed, "I *am* the princess. Princess Roza. The one who ran away, remember? I guess no one put two and two together that Kiara Santiago emerged around the same time as the princess' disappearance. Anyway, I guess I just got sick of that life. I mean, I'll never really be rid of it, but I have responsibilities as princess, and I've just been ignoring them. I can't ignore them. So I'm getting to know my people, looking into what's really wrong. It's something I've got to do." Christian nodded, "Well, princess or not, I'm proud of you. What you're doing is really cool. I wish I were a prince. Then we could be best royal friends!" Kiara snorted, "You dork!" and suddenly, there were two knocks at the door.

Christian frowned at the door, "I'll bet that's the guy who wanted the sword." Kiara gave him a look as Christian unlocked the door and opened it, and almost fainted when she saw who was at the door.

"James?" Christian cried. James smiled, "Christian! Man!" they bro-hugged and Christian let him in. "James, you remember—" Kiara was up to Christian, dragging him away before he could finish his sentence. She slammed him against a wall in another room, "Don't you dare say my name!" Christian was breathing heavily, a little shocked, "Why?" Kiara sighed, "He can't know it's me. He'll just take me back to Kinkan. Only you and my friend Calvin know my identity, got it?" Christian nodded fervently, "Yep. Got it. So who do I introduce you as?" Kiara thought. She hadn't thought about that. "Just…make something up. You're clever. Make it something not stupid or obvious, got it?" Christian nodded, "Got it."

They went back to the room calmly. James was standing there with an odd look on his face, but he didn't say anything. Christian cleared his throat, "James, I'd like you to meet my friend Ro. She's staying with me for a few months." James stuck out his hand, "Ro. Pleasure to meet you." Kiara stuck out her hand and shook his. She could see the odd look in James' eyes when he realized their hands fit together perfectly, "The pleasure's mine."

"So where's that sword?" James asked, closing the topic. Christian's face split into a wide grin, "Wait here." and he ran upstairs to grab it. James turned to Kiara, "So, Ro, how do you know Christian?" Kiara shrugged, "He and I knew each other from a group we were in together." James gave her a look, "Really? What group?" and Kiara immediately realized her mistake. James probably knew that Christian had been part of the Messengers. She had to cover herself much better than this.

"Um, yeah. One in Dorado City. I forget the name." James' face returned to normal, but still slightly disappointed, "Oh, cool." Kiara nodded, "How do you know him?" James smiled shyly, "We're both avid sword collectors. Kind of a bit of a vice, I guess. Never use them.

Just for show." Kiara gave him a look, "Then why keep them if you never use them?" James shrugged, "They're cool. I grew up with them. My family was obsessed with swords. My father loved them, had a huge collection. It's kind of like a way of connecting with them, I guess."

"And here you are, sir." Christian handed a long box to James. James smiled and handed him some coins. "Thanks, Christian. I've got to go, I'll catch you later." Kiara looked at him, "You're not even going to check the box?" Christian gaped at her, "Pardon?" James laughed, "Why? He's my friend. He wouldn't jack the box. Besides, we've traded before. I trust him. Don't you? Since you've been friends for so long. See you later guys." and he left.

Christian turned to her, hands on hips, "Okay, girl. Time to spill the whole thing. Now." Kiara looked down ashamedly and went to the living room with him. "Well...before I came here, I kind of got in a fight with James." Christian sat down, "Why?"

"Because he was being so...he was so...annoying! He was hovering and trying to tell me what to do and getting in my business and I just couldn't deal with it! I don't like that kind of stuff. And I was just so…so angry! I grabbed my daggers and he grabbed his sword and we fought, and then I just realized...I couldn't keep doing this. Fighting with people. It was so tiring, and I was so sick of being angry. I wanted happiness, and I thought I had that, but I didn't. So I ran. I didn't know what else to do. My life has always been about running. And I knew it had to stop. You know the rest."

Christian nodded, "So why can't James know it's you?" Kiara crossed her legs, "Because if he knows it's me, he'll drag me back. That's what he's here for. He's looking for me so he can take me back to Kinkan. It's just that I have this mission thing to do. I can't let anybody but you and my friend Calvin know my identity. You have to promise to keep it a secret." Christian nodded, "I promise. Of course I promise. You're my friend, Kiara." Kiara smiled sadly, "Thanks, Christian. I owe you." Christian hugged her, "You saved my life when I was younger. I'm the one who owes you."

—

James sighed, listening to Holly rage on the phone, "You saw her?" she cried, "You saw her and you let her go? What's wrong with you, Delarosa?" James sighed, exasperated. "Holly, it wasn't her. She had brown hair. And it wasn't curly. You know as well as I do that Kiara prizes her hair above all other physical features. There's no way it was her. I just mistook a girl who looked like her as Kiara. They say you have about seven people in the world who look very similar to you." he could hear Holly's annoyance, "And you bought a sword? Really? A sword?" James shrugged, "It was supposed to be sent to me, but I was in town, so I thought I'd pick it up instead of paying the extra money for it. Cut me some slack with what I get paid, okay?" Holly groaned, "You're supposed to be finding her!"

James looked to the ground, "How long do I have?" he could hear the typing of keys on a keyboard through the other end of the line, "Six months. You have six months before the next convention. We need her there, otherwise this plan won't work out." James nodded, "Six months it is." Holly sighed, "See you 'round, kid." James nodded, "Bye, Holly."

God only knows what she'd tell Root. He can already imagine his red face and his veins pulsing in his forehead. With a groan, James ran back into town. If he was going to be here for a while, he might as well look for a place to stay.

Kiara shut the door to her motel room behind her and started to grab her belongings. Calvin, who had seemed to calm down, was confused, "Where are you going?" Kiara sighed, "I'm staying with Christian. I'm going to get a job and start doing something with my life." Calvin chuckled sarcastically, "You're going to get a job? You have no experience!" Kiara looked daggers at him, and Calvin paled, "Look, buddy, I have spent my whole entire life taking care of children who needed it. I know how to work in almost any setting, especially with kids. Don't tell me there isn't some day-care center around here that could use an extra hand. And don't criticize me. In fact, why don't you just stop talking to me?" she tossed a Youan at him, and he frowned, "What's this for?" Kiara slung her bag over her shoulder and with a cold look, murmured, "The room. Thank you." and she left.

Kiara rolled her eyes and walked out into the bright sunlight. She noticed two children who were running around with sticks, playing some sort of game, who were about to be caught underneath a brown horse with a rider who wasn't paying attention.

Kiara's bag slammed to the ground as she grabbed the children and dashed to the side, shouting, "Hey!" the rider suddenly snapped out of his daydream and looked to where the shout had come from. Kiara glared at him, a man with blonde hair and crystal blue eyes.

James.

James got down and tied his horse to a fence, "I'm so sorry miss, I didn't—" he paused as he recognized her, "Ro?" Kiara looked up and prayed that James wouldn't recognize her beyond that, "Um…James, right?" she tried to lie. James smiled and stuck out his hand, "Yeah, that's right. Are you okay?" Kiara brushed herself off and suddenly remembered why she was dirty in the first place. She looked to the children, a boy and a girl, who seemed to be terrified. She went to them and crouched down, "Hey, it's alright. I've got you. You're safe."

"Lacey? Luke? Are you alright?" a frantic, pudgy woman came rushing over to them with a bushel of groceries in her arms. She set them down and went to hug the children, "Oh, thank heaven you're all right! How many times have I told you to pay attention while playing?" Kiara tapped her shoulder, "It's alright, ma'am. It wasn't their fault. This man was not paying attention while riding his horse." Kiara gestured to James, who looked to the ground, ashamed, "A thousand apologies, ma'am."

The woman huffed, "I should say so. Now, dearie, thank you for saving them! How can I ever repay you?" Kiara looked to the groceries, "Let me help you." the woman shook her head, "Nonsense! You've helped enough! How can I help you?" Kiara took the groceries anyway, "No, let me help you. Please. I'm in need of a job." the woman looked at Kiara in a scrutinizing way, "Well, you've got no muscle, you're not built for strength. Are you good with children?" Kiara nodded eagerly, "Very!" the woman smiled and touched her arm, "Come with me, then. We've got just the job for you."

James stood there as Ro was ushered off with the woman and her children. A glint from the corner of his eye made him look to the ground, where he saw a bag with a locket sticking out slightly. He recognized the locket from the night before, where he'd seen the girl with it. He picked it up, *It must belong to Ro,* but noticed something odd about it. It looked exactly like the locket that he'd given Kiara before she'd faked her death. The locket, the name, her uncanny resemblance to Kiara, it was impossible.

James looked up, but Ro and the woman and children had gone. They were lost in the sea of people.

He had to find her.

—

Calvin paced the floor of his brother's room impatiently. Where was that no-good, self-righteous idiot? He tapped his fingers against his leg and waited before finally hearing the click of a doorknob.

"Finally," he muttered to the black-cloaked being. Nicodemus snarled, "Patience, brother, patience. What is it this time?" Calvin's voice lowered, "The curse. It's wearing off." Nicodemus' eyes glinted, "What?"

Calvin shrugged, "It's your magic. You tell me. The curse is wearing off. She's becoming…kind. Good. I don't know, just not what she's supposed to be. She's got this stupid idea that she can take back the throne." Nicodemus' eyes glinted, and he glared daggers at Calvin, "What? Take back the throne? How dare she? That impudent, impertinent little wench!" he calmed himself and took a few deep breaths, sitting down in his large cushioned chair, "Well, if she wants the throne so badly, why don't we just give it to her?" Calvin was confused, "What do you mean?" Nicodemus chuckled, "Bring the others to me. I have a new plan."

Nicodemus almost chuckled. So the curse was wearing off? No doubt another one would kill her; she was too magically fragile. But what did he have to fear? She was Dark. She would turn to their side no matter what. Surely he had nothing to worry about.

Surely.

"Oof!" Kiara let out a grunt as she was tackled to the ground. She laughed heartily, "Mary-Jean! Jake! I will get you!" she stood up suddenly and began to chase the two toddlers around the park.

James spotted the woman from before, and timidly went up to her. He was not too keen on being yelled at like before. He cleared his throat, "Madam?" the woman turned around, surprised, and then angry. "What do you want?" she demanded. James took a deep, quick breath, and got down to one knee, "I would like to formally apologize for my behavior earlier. If there is anything I can do to make it up to you, please, let me know." the woman rolled her eyes, "Make it up? Almost killing two of my children and you want to make it up to me?" James persisted, "Please, ma'am. It was an honest accident. I wasn't paying attention to where I was going. I was foolish. Please, let me do something to repay you." The woman sighed and looked to the brown-haired girl who was playing with the children.

"Oh," she gave in, "all right. All right. See that girl over there? You'll be her assistant. She can't handle all of them by herself. Go now; go on!" James let out a rushed thanks and hurried over to the girl. He smiled as she noticed him, and held out her bag, "You forgot this back there." Roza looked at the bag, and back at him. She smiled slightly and took the bag, "Thank you." James bowed his head, "What shall you have me do?" Ro was confused, "I'm sorry?" James shrugged, "I'm kind of your assistant. To make up for what happened earlier." Ro nodded slowly, "Oh. Well, um, you can…why don't you go round up the children so we can go back to the orphanage?" James looked to all the clean-clothed children. He'd never thought for even a moment that they could be orphans.

Madeleine came up to Ro, who gave her employer an accusing look, "You told him to be my assistant?" Madeleine chuckled, "He wouldn't give up! Besides, you two look good together. Make some friends, why don't you? You deserve some." Madeleine's attention turned to three of the children, and she rushed away. Ro sighed. She didn't need friends, she needed to work. Having too many friends would distract her from that.

James came up to her, "So I'm not too good with children…Maddie took over." Ro looked over to Madeleine, who was leading the line, "Of course you're not. Come on, there's still lots to do. Can you cook?"

James smiled as he chopped more tomatoes and dumped them into the boiling pot of peppers, tomatoes, and spices. He was glad to be of some use, since he wasn't sure how to be firm with children. He laughed to himself, trying to imagine Ro's face when she'd been tackled. The thought filled him with warmth, her smile.

"James!" called Madeleine, always in a rush, "Is that spaghetti done yet?" James looked into the sauce. *Done!*

"Yep!" he replied, grabbing the pot with his covered hands, "Here it comes!" he brought the sauce out to the large table where the pasta and bread was set. The kids clapped and smiled widely as each of them were served. Over in the corner, Ro smiled secretly, and continued cleaning.

Once all of the children had been fed, they were sent off to bed, and Roza and James were dismissed for the day. Ro spent a few extra minutes tidying up the kitchen, and slipped out the door.

James sped after her, "Ro!" he called, "Ro, where are you going?" she pointed in the direction she was heading, "I'm going to Christian's. I'm staying with him for a while." James smiled, "Then let me walk you home. I have the apartment right next to him." silently, she agreed, and together they walked.

"So, have you lived here your whole life?" Kiara wanted to be careful with her answer. "No," she said, "I'm only here for a few more months. I'm spending a year here doing volunteer work." James nodded, "So you're a missionary or something?" Kiara smiled, "Or something."

As they neared Christian's house, James sighed, "You remind me a lot of someone I know." Kiara became tense, but she had to act dubious, "Who's that?" James opened the door to Christian's and followed her up the stairs into her room, which was very blank. It looked like no one had been in there for weeks.

"This is your room?" he commented, "It's pretty empty." Kiara had to think up a reply, "I had to clean the walls and floors, so I took everything out." she smiled nervously, trying to change the subject, "What does your room look like?" James shrugged, "Not much different, but the walls are black. I prefer dark colors." Kiara sat down on her bed, trying to discreetly shove her bag underneath it,

"Why's that?" James shrugged, "That's how it was at my old home. I grew up in a very prominent home. But you already knew that." Kiara tried to look confused, but she had a feeling that her heartbeat could be heard from a mile away.

A faraway smile came over James' face as he sat down in the chair near the window, "You remind me very much of someone I know. Her name is Kiara. She's one of the most incredible people I've ever met." Kiara's breathing stopped for a moment as she tried not to blush. James stood up and looked at her, "She's daring and smart, she knows what she wants and doesn't stop until she has it; she's harsh and doesn't like to get too close to people, and she's always looking out for others before herself. Recently, though, she ran away. We have this weird relationship, see. I'm in love with her, and I'm pretty sure she loves me, but she's too scared to admit it." James slowly walked closer and closer towards Kiara, but she was frozen in her spot. She was terrified. What should she do? Run, or stay?

Before she had time to decide, James had closed the space between them so that their bodies were almost touching. He looked down at her with soft eyes, "She's the most beautiful girl I've ever seen in my entire life. And she looks just as beautiful with brown hair." James cupped Kiara's cheek and pressed his lips to hers.

Kiara was surprised, but she didn't fight back. She reached up and spread her fingers through his hair and felt his muscular back. James' hands wandered along her waist and neck and back, and soon they were tangled up in each other. They moved together towards the bed where James sat down with Kiara on his lap. He gripped her waist fiercely as their kisses became more and more passionate. His hand skimmed her hair as Kiara drew tiny designs on his back, pulling him closer and closer with each stroke.

James stood and pressed her down onto the bed, lying gently next to her. He pushed himself up and touched her lips with his, soft at first, but soon their kisses were urgent. Kiara's lips blazed with fire and her hands and body coursed with electricity as they ran over James' body and collided with him. James sighed into her neck and began to kiss her cheeks, her forehead, her ears, her neck, her collarbone.

"Hey, Kiara, I—" a voice from the doorway paused abruptly. Kiara and James sprung up and saw Christian, slack-jawed and shocked in the doorway. They looked at each other and Kiara suddenly cried, "What are you doing? Get away from me!" as she pushed him.

James was confused, and he tried to speak, but Christian beat him to it, "So I'm going to take a wild guess and say that I don't have to call you Ro around him?" James almost laughed, "I would guess not." Christian backed up slightly, "I'll, um, leave you two be. If you need anything, like, you know, condoms and stuff, they're in the—"

"CHRISTIAN!" Kiara shouted as Christian laughed and ran away.

Kiara cleared her throat and looked to James, shaking her head, "How did you know?" James shrugged, "You're not that good at keeping secrets from me." he sighed and rubbed his hands through his hair in frustration, "Kiara...why? Why do you keep running from me?"

Kiara shrugged and stood up, "I don't know. Love just...doesn't work out for me." James stood with her, "You told me that, but...please. Give me a chance. Please." Kiara stood by the window, "And what happens if it doesn't work out? What happens if you begin to hate me?" James laughed and put a hand on her arm, "I've been chasing you for years. I've seen you at your worst, and your best. There is nothing that you could ever do to make me hate you. That I promise you." Kiara turned around and looked at him, her face uncertain and fearful.

James gave her a reassuring smile, "I love you, Kiara. There is nothing you could ever do or say to change the way I feel about you." he gave Kiara another kiss, and another.

And another.

CHAPTER 10:

Christian knocked on Kiara's door and opened it slightly, "Kiara—" he was cut off by James pulling his shirt on and closing the door behind him, "Shh! She's still sleeping." Christian looked at him with amusement, "Nice hair." James rolled his eyes and went into the kitchen, grabbing some milk.

"I'm going to kill you for not telling me," he commented, pouring himself a glass. Christian threw up his hands, "She threatened to do the same to me if I did tell you! And I take her threats much more seriously." Christian sat down, "So how'd it go?" James shrugged, "Well, it wasn't like I didn't know. I just couldn't believe she was trying that hard to pretend she didn't know me. What did I do?" Christian sighed, "Look, I've known her for a long time. She likes her space. She likes her independence. She values her freedom above anything else. When you start hovering...she gets defensive."

James ran his fingers through his hair, "I never meant to hover. I just...I didn't want anything to happen to her." Christian nodded and poured himself some cereal, "Yeah, I get that, but Kiara's tough. Beyond tough. She's more than capable of handling herself. She doesn't want someone to protect her." He sat down across from James and looked him in the eyes, "She wants a partner. An equal. Someone who will let her thrive. She needs that. She can't be...caged up."

James nodded, "Yeah. I get it." Christian smiled with a mouthful of oats, "Good. So, how did the relationship talk go?" James slumped down in his chair, defeated, "I don't know, to be honest. She's so afraid. And I don't know whether she's afraid of being hurt or hurting others or both, but she thinks that the solution is to just close herself off from people." Christian shrugged, "Can you blame her? She's had no emotional stability ever. Like, never ever. She's been handed from place to place, lost family after family...it's no wonder she doesn't trust people." James nodded and sat down next to him, "Yeah, I know. I just wish she'd give me a chance." Christian snorted, "What reason does she have to give anyone a chance? Give me one and then I'll accept your plea."

"Hi, guys." A sleepy Kiara walked into the kitchen and grabbed the orange juice. Christian laughed, "Good morning, sunshine. So, you and James, what exactly did you end up doing last—" James punched him in the shoulder hard enough to shut him up, but Christian kept laughing at Kiara's red face.

"Okay, okay." he chuckled, "So, what are the plans for today?" Kiara looked to the ground in thought, "I'm going to see my grandmother." James and Christian were both confused, "Your grandmother?" James questioned. Kiara nodded, "Yeah. She's my real mother's mom. I met her when I was on the way here. I'm going to see her again." Christian stood up, "We'll come with you." James stood with him and shot Christian a look, "But only if you want us to." Kiara nodded, not looking at them, "No, it's okay. We're not coming back here anyway. We leave in an hour. Be prepared to walk a distance."

Hours later, Christian was complaining. "How much further?" he whined. Kiara sighed and turned around, standing up on her tiptoes and grabbing his collar, pulling him down to her height, "I have spent my entire life training and running and fighting, and you're complaining about a two hour walk?" Christian looked to the ground, "Complain? Pssh! No, I was just…" with another look into Kiara's intense green eyes, he nodded sheepishly, "Yep. Got it." Kiara nodded and let him go, leading the way once again. James snickered at Christian, and gave him a light shove. Christian shoved him back twice as hard with a red face.

"Well, here we are." Kiara started to walk up to a small house with a well in the front. James looked at her questionably, "This is your grandmother's house?" Kiara nodded, "Yeah. Got a problem?" James shook his head, "Nothing, it's just…I stopped by this woman's house and talked to her before I went to Jinora. She's the one who told me to go there." Kiara slapped her forehead, "Of course. Why wouldn't you? And of course that's how you found me. I should've guessed." Kiara knocked at the door and stepped back, waiting patiently.

An elderly lady opened the door and smiled, "My dear! You're back so soon! And you've brought friends!" Kiara hugged the woman, "Hello, Grandmother." Mabel looked at her in confusion, "Pardon?" Kiara shook her head, "Why don't we go inside?" Mabel smiled, "Yes, come in! I've just made stew!"

"So," Mabel sat down once everyone had been served, "what's this 'grandmother' business?" Kiara put her spoon down and looked at her, "My mother's name was Kasimira, my father's Sean. They were the former king and queen of Lodos. I have a twin brother named Rowan. We were born on an island to the South. When my parents were killed, I was sent to live with King Garren and Queen Ana. You told me about your daughter, Kassi, who lived in an island to the South, who had twins. She died when they were babies and they were sent to live with important people up North. It didn't take much for me to figure it out." Mabel stood up and pulled Kiara up with her, "You never told me your name." she whispered. Kiara took a deep, shaky breath, "It's Roza." Kiara cried out in surprise when the seemingly feeble woman pulled her into a strong hug. She laughed and hugged her back.

Mabel sniffed and let her go, "Where's Rowan?" Kiara looked at James, who shrugged, "We're assuming he either went back to the castle or to his studies. We haven't heard differently." Kiara nodded, "Good, then we might run into him." Christian was confused, "What do you mean?" Kiara looked at her grandmother, "I can't keep delaying everything. I have to go back to the castle. These are my people. I have a duty to take care of them." James stood and put a hand on her shoulder, "That's great, Kiara, but how do you know they'll even accept you? You said it yourself, the Dark Faelis…they wouldn't like it." Kiara shook her head, "I don't know. But I have to try."

"What are you going to do about Nicodemus though, if you're running the kingdom?" Christian questioned. At the mention of that name, Mabel glared daggers at him, "Who?" Christian visibly shrunk, "Um…Nicodemus…the guy who killed Kiara's parents and who wants to get rid of her…right?" he looked to Kiara, who nodded, remembering the story she'd confided in him. Mabel chuckled sarcastically, "You leave that incompetent fool to me." Christian smiled and whispered to Kiara, "I like this lady." Kiara shook her head in amusement and turned to her grandmother, "Incompetent fool? You know who he is?" Mabel laughed, "Of course I do. We were…lovers of sorts in the past." Kiara almost fell down. She couldn't believe what had just come out of her mouth. James and Christian sat down, visibly shocked.

"What? Your boyfriend was Nicodemus?" Kiara couldn't believe it. Mabel shrugged, "He wasn't always like that. He changed his appearance and became bitter after his family's tragedy. After that, he was never the same, and we parted ways." James took the bowls from the table and helped Mabel with the dishes, "So what happened to his family?" Mabel looked at him pointedly, "Your parents believed his family to be capable of Dark magic—which they were—and had his family killed for the crime." James was confused, "Wait, you knew my parents?" Mabel rolled her eyes, "Sonny, I was queen of this land years ago. Of course I knew them! Anyway, Nicodemus escaped and declared that he would destroy your family, but not by killing them. He would destroy everything they loved, like they'd done to him. When your family was killed, that left you, your brother, and your sister, and he was determined to take everything from you. That means her." she looked to Kiara, "Dear, he isn't after you just because you're the Faelis, he's after you because you mean a great deal to this man." she pointed to James.

James put down the dry bowls, "But what about Justin? And Anna?" Mabel half-shrugged, "Well, Justin only cares about his studies, and Anna disappeared. He has nothing left." James was confused, "How do you know she disappeared?" Mabel raised her eyebrows, "Well, it's not exactly a secret. For years there were posters of her all over. It didn't take long to figure out. I know a great deal more than I let on, you know."

"What if Anna didn't disappear?" Christian piped up. The three looked at him, "What?" they asked collectively. Christian rapped his knuckles on the table, "Well, I was thinking…you said that Anna disappeared when you were coming to Lodos, right?" James nodded, "Yeah." Christian shrugged, "Well, what if he took her? Kidnapping your sister to hurt you? He obviously knew you'd blame yourself. Doesn't it make sense?" James and Kiara looked to Mabel, who nodded, "He could be very right." James grabbed Kiara's bag and shoved it to her chest, kissing the woman on her cheek and grabbing Christian, "Well, it was great seeing you again. We're going to go to Nicodemus' castle now. Come on."

Kiara pulled back, "Whoa, whoa, whoa! We don't even know if he does. When I was there, I never heard of any other prisoners." James turned to her, his eyes ablaze, "We have to try! If there's even a remote possibility that she could be there…" Kiara nodded, "I know. But we can't just jump in there unprepared. We need backup." James cocked his head at her mischievous smile, "Backup?"

"Guys?" James opened the door to the L.P.D., and was no sooner in the door when he was ambushed by his friends. "James!" cried Rose, leaping into a hug. She kissed him on the cheek and looked over to Christian and Kiara. "You brought her back!" she exclaimed, crushing Kiara with all her might. She whispered into Kiara's ear, "If you ever run away again, I will kill you." and pulled away, smiling at her. Kiara cleared her throat nervously, "Got it."

"Who's this?" Rose questioned Kiara. Kiara stood between Christian and Rose, "Rose, this is Christian, a former member of the Messengers and a friend of James'. Christian, this is my best friend, Rose." Rose took his extended hand and shook it, "Pleased to meet you." she said shyly. Christian smiled softly, "The pleasure is all mine, believe me." Kiara rolled her eyes and gagged, looking to Holly, Root, Gabriel, and Felix, who were having words with James. "Look, guys," she interrupted, "I don't mean to break up this tea party, but we're going back to Nicodemus' castle." Holly narrowed her eyes, contemplating whether or not she was serious, "What? Why? We have business to finish with you!"

Kiara sighed, "Because there's a chance that James' sister Anna could be there. If she is, we're going to find her, and we won't do it alone. So come on, you can finish with me later." Holly shook her head, "And if she's not?" James looked down to Holly, "And if she's not, then we'll know that it's one less place we need to look." Holly sighed, but nodded, "You're lucky I like you so much. Let's go."

—

As they neared the castle, Felix spoke up, "So what, we're just going to knock on the front door and say, 'Oh, hello, we're looking for a girl named Anna that you may or may not have captured just less than ten years ago?" Kiara rolled her eyes, "Funny. No, you idiot. We're going to sneak in the back, the same way we got out. I sent Rowan an owl, he should be here by—"

"There you guys are!" Rowan appeared suddenly behind Kiara, who jumped out of her skin. The rest of the group tried their hardest not to laugh as Kiara turned around furiously to her brother, "What the hell do you think you're doing? You scared me half to death!" Rowan snickered, "Well, at least it was only half to death. Couldn't have you dead, now could we? There would be no one left to tease." Before she could reply, he looked to the turrets of the castle, "Come on, let's go before some scout sees us."

and Kiara, holding back another smart remark, followed him with the rest of them.

Climbing up the rock wall proved to be a lot easier than climbing down it, and in no time, they were back in the dungeons.

"Doesn't this bring back great memories?" Rowan asked, putting on a cheerfully sarcastic demeanor. When he was given a dry look by the rest of them, he nodded, "Okay, okay. So I think I have an idea."

As they headed silently up the stairs, Rowan explained to them, "When we were here, I would spend my evenings after supper wandering around. I would always hear laughing coming from a room that was locked. It was odd to me, so I tried to inquire with Excalibur what was going on. He said that he honestly didn't know, but had been told to never go in that room, ever. He said Nicodemus got really mad when he asked about it. I know Excalibur isn't exactly the definition of trustworthy, but I think he was telling the truth." Kiara nodded, "So we're supposed to break into a locked room, maybe find a person, and get out of there without Nicodemus seeing or hearing us?" Rowan rolled his eyes as they passed a mirror, "Look into the mirror."

Kiara shook her head, "I see nothing." and then her eyes widened with realization, "I see nothing! What the hell is going on?" Rowan shrugged, "A little coverage spell. You didn't honestly think I was that stupid, did you?" Kiara shrugged back, "Wouldn't put it past you." Rowan rolled his eyes and was about to make a remark back when Holly interrupted, "Look, I know we're invisible and all, but unless you can make us mute to everyone else, I suggest you *keep it down*!" Rowan and Kiara nodded together silently, but continued to glare at each other.

"This is it," Rowan whispered, "this is the room." he looked at the door and nodded to Kiara, who took out a pin from her pocket and jiggled it inside the lock until it gave way. Looking back to the gang, she gave them each their job, "Gabriel, Felix, guard the door. If anyone comes, you've got to warn Holly and Root who will be right inside the door listening. Rowan, you and James will come with me to look for whoever's possibly in here."

With nods from everyone else, Kiara opened the door, tailed by James and Rowan. The room was a large, cream-colored circle with light purple tapestries hanging from the ceiling. There were pretty chests full of dresses and tiaras and stuffed animals and makeup. Pillows and blankets were strewn all over the room, and in the corner, there was a small bed with a purple canopy hanging over it. Inside the canopy, there was a young girl, startled, looking at the open door. Rowan whispered an incantation, and the girl's eyes widened even more. She could now see them.

"Who are you?" her high-pitched voice called. Kiara looked to James and nodded. He stepped forward, "My name is James. Who are you?" the girl stepped out of the purple curtains, and the three of them could see her clearly now. She had long, wavy dirty-blonde hair. Her eyes were crystal blue, and her button nose was splashed with freckles. She was the spitting image of James.

"I'm Anna." She paused, "I don't want to leave," she protested softly, "this is my home." James came closer to her, "What do you remember about your childhood, Anna?" Anna backed up slightly and shrugged, "Not much. I remember fire. And then I woke up here. Master has been taking care of me ever since." James furrowed his brow, "Master? Taking care of you? How?" Anna gestured to the room, "He gave me a room, clothes, food, toys, lessons, anything I wanted."

"And what did you give him in return?" Anna shook her head, "Nothing, if I would call him Master and do as he asked." Kiara stepped forward, "What did he ask of you?" Anna sat on her bed, "Mostly cleaning. Sometimes he would ask me to be a servant to the guests." James tried to calm down. He couldn't blow up in front of her, not in this fragile state."

"Anna," James knelt down in front of her, "do you have a mirror?" Anna nodded and stood, crossing the room and removing a purple cloth from a standing mirror. James took her arms and stood next to her in front of it. At first, Anna looked confused, but as she stared at their reflections, her face became more and more shocked. Eventually, she backed away from him, "You look like me," she said.

James laughed, "Technically, since I was born first, you look like me." Anna put her hands on her head, "Born first? I don't understand." James sighed, "Anna, it's me. It's

Martin. Your brother." Anna's eyes widened and she backed up, running into her desk, "No. I have no family." James nodded, "Yes. You do. When you were little, our home was attacked. Our mother put us on a horse to come to Lodos where it was safe, but I turned around and you were gone. I haven't seen you since. Nicodemus stole you from me. I've spent my whole life looking for you."

Rowan put a hand on his shoulder, "Okay, I think you're freaking her out. Let me take this from here." James reluctantly stepped back, and Rowan took Anna's arms, "I know this is a lot to take in, and I know you don't think it's true, but you have to believe us. That man, your brother, has dedicated his life's work in looking for you. You've got to give us a chance." Anna sat down, "But Master told me—" Kiara stepped in, "Your master is an evil genius. He's spent the good portion of his life trying to kill and hurt people, he even tried to use my brother and I for our powers. We spent a while here, too. He lied to you. We're sorry." Anna looked at Rowan, "Are you sure you have the right person?" Rowan looked to James, who kneeled in front of her, "You are my sister. My flesh and blood. I'd know you anywhere."

"Guys, emergency! Nicodemus!" James, Holly, Root, and Kiara looked to Rowan, who whispered the spell to make them invisible again. They all pressed up against the walls. Anna sat down on her bed and pretended to busy herself with a drawing.

"Anna?" the door opened, and Nicodemus walked in. His face, normally hidden, was fully exposed. His eyes were an orange color, his skin raw and crinkled with burns and scars. Anna stood up, "Hello, Master." Nicodemus smiled, "How is my flower doing today?" Anna smiled and sat down, "I'm well." Nicodemus patted her head, "Good."

"Master," Anna questioned cautiously, "why am I here with you?" Nicodemus looked at her questionably, "Why do you ask that?" Anna shrugged, "I'm fourteen now, almost fifteen. I don't want to be locked in here anymore. I want to see the world, to make friends. I want to know where I come from." Nicodemus stood angrily, "What is the meaning of this? Have I not given you everything you've ever asked, everything you could hope for? Have I not cared for you when your family abandoned you?" Anna was shocked, "Abandoned?"

Nicodemus sighed, "Abandoned. Your brother left you for dead. I took you in when no one wanted you." Anna sat down in shock, "I have a brother?" Nicodemus snorted, "You have two. No-good, rotten things, the lot of them. They've never looked for you, never cared for you. I care for you. You should be grateful. You are mine. Do you understand?" Anna nodded feebly, "Yes, Master. I understand. Thank you." Nicodemus sighed, "Good girl." and with a swish of his cloak, he left.

Rowan whispered the reverse incantation and gave a look to Anna, who stood up and went to James, touching his face softly, "I don't remember you." James, with tears in his eyes, shook his head, "That's okay. I remember you."

Kiara rolled her eyes, "Hey, guys, I hate to break this up, but can we do this later? Let's get out of here!" Rowan nodded, "Let's go."

The eight figures walked out of the room silently and slipped down the stairs. Nicodemus was nowhere to be found, but Excalibur and Calvin crossed their path.

"I can't believe you let her go, you idiot." Excalibur was fuming. Calvin rolled his eyes, "It wouldn't be my problem if you'd done a better job the first time." Excalibur whipped around, slapping Calvin in the face, "Shut up! I had to handle the both of them. That Light Faelis has been trained for years to be the most knowledgeable sorcerer on the planet. You had to handle the fighter! A fighter! A girl who's only hobby is hurting others. You let your emotions get in the way. You were soft."

Calvin stood still, "Well at least I didn't fall in love with her." Excalibur stopped in his tracks, and the rest of the seven looked to Kiara, whose face was white as a sheet. Excalibur went closer to Calvin, "Manipulation. That's what it's called. That damn girl wouldn't know what love was if it hit her in the face. She's Dark. She's not capable of it. You should have seen Victor before we gave him the serum. He would have followed her into hell if she'd asked him to."

Kiara looked to the ground. Victor loved her? She looked to James, whose face was saddened. He started walking forward, leading the group away from the brothers, and out of the castle.

Anna gawked at all of the new places as they headed to the police department's building. James couldn't stop looking and smiling at her. He couldn't stop crying, either.

"Well, this is your stop," Kiara motioned to the others, keeping Rowan by her side. James was confused, "Our stop? What do you mean?" Kiara and Rowan looked to each other, "We've been thinking," Rowan started, "and it's time we go and run our kingdom." James smiled at Kiara, "That's great! Let's go!" Kiara backed up, "No, I mean us. As in Rowan and I. You need to stay here." James was confused, "I don't understand. You don't want me to come with you?" Kiara shook her head, "Your life is here. Mine's not anymore." James sighed and looked to Anna, "No, my life isn't here. My life is back in Alacrast, where we belong. It's time for Justin to rule, and we need to help him." Anna smiled, "I get to meet them?" James threw up his hands, "Of course you get to meet them, they're your family!"

Kiara looked to James and smiled softly, "Well, we'll see you." James nodded and gave her a hug, "I love you." he said out loud, loud enough for everyone to hear. The gang froze, waiting for Kiara's response. She nodded, "Bye, James."

———

"Halt! Who goes there?" Kiara and Rowan stood at the gate and held hands, reassuring one another.

"Princess Roza and Prince Rowan!" called Rowan confidently. When one of the guards came to inspect them, his eyes widened, "It's them!" he called excitedly, "It's them! Lift the gates! Alert the royal family!" Kiara took a deep breath and tried to calm her stomach, which was twisting and churning with anxiety.

"Hey," Rowan squeezed her hand, "it'll be okay." Kiara nodded and smiled thankfully at him, and they walked into the grand reception room. Kiara looked around, pleased with the familiarity of her once home. The reception hall was still decked in white and gold marble with thick, red curtains. There was even a dent where Kendall had once hit the wall with his sword, chipping the marble.

"Roza?" a call from behind them came. Kiara and Rowan turned around to see Ana and Garren, staring unbelievingly at the twins. Kiara held up her hands, "Garren…Ana, I can explain—" but was cut off by their sudden embraces. Ana sniffled, "Oh, my sweet girl," she whispered, "we thought you were dead." Kiara was stunned, "You're…you're not mad? You don't hate me?" Ana let her go, "Of course not," she choked, "you're our girl. We love you. Kendall told us." Garren embraced her fiercely, and Kiara laughed, "Well, it's going to take a lot more than a couple of assassins to kill me." she reassured her, muffled by Garren's chest. Garren, unlike Ana, had trouble keeping his composure.

Finally, the king pulled away and sniffed away his tears, "Well, come on now, let's get your brothers and sisters together. And let's hear what's happened to you." Kiara nodded, "Of course. But before that, Rowan and I have an announcement." Ana and Garren exchanged confused glances, but waited patiently for their response.

"We've decided that we wish to take over the kingdom." Ana and Garren's facial expressions quickly changed from confusion to shock, and back to confused. "When?" questioned Ana. Rowan shrugged, "As soon as possible." Garren stepped forward, "So you intend to be king and queen of this land?" Kiara sighed and shook her head, and then all three of the others were confused. Kiara stepped back, "No, Garren. Rowan will be king, and when the time comes, he will have a queen." Rowan was baffled, "What? But you said—" Kiara nodded, "I know. But I don't belong here. I need to actually be doing something to better this kingdom. I've decided to turn the Messengers into a nonprofit organization. And I need to take care of Nicodemus. He has Victor. I've no doubt his plans haven't stopped." Ana and Garren shook their heads and asked at the same time, "Messengers?" Ana continued, "The illegal ring of runaways?" Kiara shook her head, "It's not illegal, and they're not all runaways. They're good kids who need someone who cares. I care about them. Rowan cares about this country. It's only fitting."

Rowan hugged his sister, "That is the best thing I've ever heard you say." Kiara hugged him back and turned to her guardians, "I'm afraid I can't stay. But I will join you at the coronation. Rowan will let me know when it is. I have things I need to attend to." King Garren motioned for a guard, "Fetch me a pardoning document." the guard nodded, "Right away, sir." Kiara was confused, "Pardoning document?" Garren sighed, "I can't imagine you did everything legally all those years. I'm pardoning you so you can take care of these kids." Kiara smiled, and said nothing. Rather, she didn't know what to say.

"I, King Garren of Lodos," he spoke as he wrote, "hereby pardon Princess Roza Kiara Collins of all crimes committed to the people and republic of Lodos, et cetera, et cetera…" at the bottom, he stamped the royal seal and signed his name. He rolled the parchment up and handed it to Kiara, hugging her, "Good luck, sweet Roza. We shall see you in a few weeks." Kiara hugged Ana and Rowan one last time, and as she walked out the doors, she looked back at her smiling family and waved.

—

"I present to you, King Rowan Seamus Collins of Lodos." the room erupted in applause and Rowan stood and turned around, smiling at his now subjects, looking ever so regal in his red garb.

Once the guests had moved themselves to the ballroom, Kiara hesitated in going. Rowan put a hand on her shoulder, "You okay?" Kiara looked at him, trying to look like she wasn't nervous, "Of course, yes, it's just that...the last time I was in that ballroom someone tried to kill me." Rowan laughed, "Well, you're much better equipped to handle it now. Come on, let's go have some fun. We have guests to greet, Lady Princess." Kiara snorted, "Yes, Lord King."

Kiara stepped into the ballroom and couldn't help but smile at the golden light, much like the night she ran away. Funny to think that the reason she left and the reason she came back—a party—were the same.

"May I have this dance?" Kiara turned around, surprised to see James. "James," she cried with joy, "you're here!" James nodded, "The princes and princess of Alacrast wouldn't miss this for the world. Besides, I had to see you again, now that you're so busy with the new Messengers, or what is it called?" Kiara laughed, "Children of Lodos." James smiled, "Right, that." Kiara hugged him, "I've missed you." James hugged her back, "I've missed you, too."

Kiara looked over to Rowan, who was dancing with Anna, and blushing, "It seems my brother has made an impression on your sister." James rolled his eyes, amused, "He already asked me permission to date her." Kiara raised her eyebrows, "What did you say?" James shrugged, "I told him it was up to her, but if he hurt her, you might have to take over." Kiara laughed, "Good choice of words. I'm surprised you kept your restraint."

As they danced, James looked into her eyes sincerely, "Kiara, can I ask you something?" Kiara nodded, "Of course." when she saw his smile fade, she became concerned. James sighed, "What happened between you and Victor?" Kiara stepped back abruptly, "What? Nothing. Nothing ever happened between us. We just…we were close. Very close. And now Nicodemus has him." James sighed, "You know…I just want you to be happy." Kiara nodded, "I know. I just can't have another person in my life right now. I have to sort things out first." James nodded back, "I understand. So what are your plans now?" Kiara sighed, "I don't know. I have to find out a way to get in there and find out what's going on."

Rowan, with Anna, came over to the partners, "What are you two moping over here for? Come on! Grandma's here! And I think Rose and Christian might have just kissed…" Kiara snorted, "Of course. Alright, alright, we're coming." James and Kiara followed Rowan and Anna, laughing, over to the rest of their friends. Kiara smiled and looked around her. She had her family back, friends she could count on, and James. If only Victor and Tallah were there.

Kiara's smile slowly faded.

Victor…

—

"Damn those kids!" Nicodemus slammed his fist into the table, knocking over the goblets of wine. Excalibur and Calvin shrugged, "She's ridiculously smart," Excalibur remarked, "your plan failed." Nicodemus glared at him, "Don't you think I understand that? I don't care that they're gone, I don't need them. They took the girl! I needed *her*!" Calvin rolled his eyes, "What's so special about a little nobody, anyway?" Nicodemus laughed sarcastically and placed a hand on his brother's throat, "Leverage, you idiot, leverage! As long as I had her, my next plan would have worked out seamlessly!"

"Well, what do you plan to do now?" Excalibur asked, bored with his brother's outbursts. Nicodemus breathed out sharply, "I'll have to use the children sooner than I thought. No doubt they're going to increase their investigation now. We'll have to move up the date." Calvin was confused, "But the hazing can only be done on a blue moon, right? How are we—" Nicodemus cut him off, "Then we'll just have to use magic, won't we? Now someone, start making that potion!" The brothers bowed, "Yes, sir."

This time, Nicodemus swore, those incessant Faelis' would not get in his way. He would rule Lodos and Alacrast. He would. *Just you wait.*